Stories I Can't Show My Mother

Ann Tinkham

First Edition
Published by Napili Press

ISBN: 978-0-9990157-1-1 (Paperback)
ISBN: 978-0-9990157-4-2 (eBook)

Cover Design: Jessica Bell.

This book is a work of fiction. Names, characters, places, and events are a product of the author's imagination. Any resemblance to actual persons, living or dead, is purely coincidental.

Visit the author website at anntinkham.com

Contents

Direct Deposit

I f someone had told Lilly as a girl, dreaming of the family she would one day have, that she would be shopping for the father of her child at a sperm bank, she would have told them they were off their rocker. But after no serendipitous meetings with Mr. Right by the age of 38, and after encountering losers, players, stalkers, and lurkers while internet dating, Lilly turned to friends.

Her friend, Felix the animation artist, responded to her request with blushing gratitude, "I'm flattered that you would ask," he said as an eclipse overtook his shiny eyes. "But I'm morally opposed to reproducing. I'm making a conscious choice to commit genetic suicide."

Lilly was silenced in the face of gene pool extinction.

Next, she asked her friend, Sage, the jazz musician/pothead. She had concerns about the effect of THC on his genes, but she asked anyway. Sage said he would happily donate (au natural—no turkey basters) if she didn't care that there were schizophrenics on every branch of his family tree.

Lilly imagined a family tree rotting from the inside out, and said, "Never mind."

Her last hope among her friends was Adam, a striking rocket scientist. He had been responsible for the Deep Impact Mission—a space project in which an impactor spacecraft penetrated a comet's nucleus. Who better than a deep impact rocket scientist to penetrate her ovum? He declined, saying under his breath that he had retrograde ejaculation—his semen didn't go through the proper channels, but instead went into his bladder. He daily pissed out the treasures from his family jewels.

Disheartened, Lilly told her girlfriends that genetic suicide, schizophrenics, and retrograde ejaculation were thwarting her attempts at sprouting an egg. They sprang into action. Rosie, Anna, and Lauren became sperm donor missionaries—approaching guys working in natural food markets, corner bars, and cafes. One intentionally bald barista with a soul patch agreed, but then confessed to low-motility sperm. He said his slow-mo swimmers drove his wife into the bed of another man. Lilly didn't want to mess around; she wanted bull's-eye turbo-sperm.

Lilly's ova were sending SOS signals to her brain—use us or lose us! The panic set in. There was only one thing left to do.

Go to the bank.

This was Lilly's second appointment with the sperm bank—Pacific TechCare, high tech with a soft touch. The first appointment had been a meet and greet.

She still had so many questions. As she made her way off the elevator, she was trying to narrow her focus. This week's assignment had been to zero in on the ideal donor profile. Otherwise, she'd be choosing between Latvian, Swedish, Northern Indian, Ashkenazi Jewish, Polish, Scottish, Peruvian, Mexican, Norwegian, English, Shoshone, Québécois, and Blackfoot sperm. Among others.

Lilly was leaning toward Québécois, because she liked the way it sounded. She could imagine the auditory seduction each time she discussed her child's genetic make-up. Of course, Shoshone or Blackfoot would allow her child to claim a minority background, which would afford him or her access to scholarships. Her head spun, trying to picture her genes combined with each of the sperm donor profiles.

When Lilly arrived, the receptionist was on a headset phone talking to a sperm donor. She was a bouncing buxom blonde with peek-a-boo cleavage and non-stop perkiness. Lilly wondered if they didn't hire her to help the donors with their deposits.

"Two to three days before your appointment, you must ejaculate to clear out your pipes—the dead sperm and debris, followed by abstinence until the time of the collection, which helps you build up your sperm count!" Miss Perky took out a mirror from her pocketbook and reapplied her strawberry-red lipstick while saying, "You can either book the collection room here, which I'd be happy to do for you, or collect at home and drop off your sample within four hours. Any longer, and the little guys go belly up. If you collect at home, you can pick up a sterile container from the lab, or use a sterilized baby food jar, as long as it's absolutely dry because water kills the swimmers. Okey-dokey?" She said this as though she were talking about fuzzy bunnies.

As Lilly listened, she couldn't help but feel she was eavesdropping on phone porn with a clinical bent. She pretended to leaf through *Golf Digest* as Miss Perky delivered her collection instructions. Out of the corner of her eye, Lilly noticed Miss Perky's screen saver; it was a soothing blue-and-white pattern. After a few seconds, she realized that the white pattern was a school of tiny sperm, tails waving as they swam across the screen.

Miss Perky ended her phone conversation. "Miss Cochran, I'll let Bridget know you're here." Miss Perky buzzed Lilly's counselor, Bridget.

Bridget appeared, dressed in red plaid from head to toe. She even sported a plaid Oliver Twist hat. Bridget was British and had been transferred from a London-based sperm bank to this one in Seattle. She was someone who wasn't afraid to use words such as "masturbation," "ejaculation," and "sperm count." The words sounded a little less obscene when said with a British accent.

"Good day, Lilly. Let's go have a look at our catalogue. Shall we?" Then as they turned the corner on the way to her office, Bridget asked, "Have you identified your ideal profile?"

"Not really. It's such a daunting task."

"Right-o. Not a problem. We'll pick out the perfect bloke in no time. You and I will chat, and then I'll send you home with a fresh-off-the-press copy of the donor catalogue. It's particularly sizzling this go-around." Bridget stopped suddenly, touched Lilly on the shoulder, and said in a whisper, "We have some celeb sperm! Can you believe it?" Bridget clapped her hands in glee. "Of course, we don't know who. I can only imagine—Denzel Washington was up here shooting a film recently. You could do a lot worse than Denzel."

Lilly was amazed by the contagious exuberance that filled the hallways and offices of the sperm bank. She would even dare say it was downright orgiastic. Lilly snickered when she realized it was the only product she knew that required an orgasm for the production process.

Bridget led Lilly to her office and offered her a seat in front of the desk. Bridget took a seat behind her expansive cherry desk. Her red plaid ensemble went well with the cherry-colored wood of her office. She set her elbows on her desk, clasped her hands together, and said, "Lilly, let me in on your thinking process."

After Bridget framed it like that, Lilly was embarrassed not to be able to reveal a sophisticated decision-making process. "Well, to tell you the truth, I've mostly been thinking I want to avoid losers who are, you know, depositing to pay the bills."

"Lilly, let me reassure you. We are not a jack-off-for-cash joint. We are the best sperm bank in the world. You're getting the highest-quality product available to donees. Alright, let me see if I can help you think this through. When you imagine a child's face you could love, what do you see?"

"I suppose I could love any child's face."

Like a teacher who received the wrong response to a question, Bridget's face sagged in disappointment. "Lilly, this is not the Peace Corps. The world of men is at your fingertips. Dream big! You don't want a carrot top with a piggly-wiggly nose and an underbite. Now do you?"

"I wouldn't mind. I'm really more concerned about personality than anything. I wish I could meet the guy—if only for a few minutes—to see if he has a sunny disposition and a smile that lights up the room."

"OK. How about this angle? Do you want Bill Gates—a brainy software magnate? Or do you want Stephen Curry—a beautiful bronze athlete? What about Colin Jost—handsome, boyish, confident, and funny? How about a literary or artistic genius? You just have to make sure you get a genius who's not crackers."

"I don't suppose any of those guys have donated. Have they?"

"Well, I'm not at liberty to say, but I'm trying to stimulate your imagination—get you to dream big."

Dream big about sperm? Bridget seemed frustrated with Lilly's inability to focus on the perfect male specimen. But Lilly just couldn't figure out how to narrow down infinite genetic possibilities.

"Alright, let's start from the top and work our way down. What color hair is your favorite?"

"I suppose blonde, red, or light brown."

"That narrows it down. If you had to choose, which would it be?"

"Blonde."

"Good. OK. Eyes—slanted, straight, wide, narrow?"

"Straight and wide."

Bridget was taking notes. "Right. Nose—wide, narrow, flat, turned up, turned down, hooked?"

"Oh, definitely not hooked. Thin and turned up."

"Excellent. Lips—full, thin?"

"Full, I guess."

"Cleft or no cleft?"

"No cleft."

"Tall or short?"

"Short if it's a girl; tall if it's a boy."

"OK. We'll go with medium, then. Alright, Lilly, we have a profile for you. You've chosen my people—Northern Europeans. The Viking clan—a hearty breed, but a bit reserved. Let's just hope you don't get a repressed bloke. I don't fancy those uptight, quiet chaps. But no worries. You can read the personal comments section. I have to warn you, though. The comments are a hybrid of bad high school essays and cheesy personal ads."

"So..." Lilly hesitated, feeling flustered and flushed. "Um, how..."

"Yes?" Bridget put her pen down and looked up at Lilly.

"Can you tell me where the restroom is?"

"Oh, I thought you were going to ask me something else. The nearby restroom is simply dreadful—the toilets are overflowing. You'll have to go to the staff restroom. Just ignore the silly sights in the hallway. It's down the hall, through the double doors, to the right, and straight back. If you go to the left, you'll end up in Donor Hall."

Silly sights?

Lilly made her way down the hallway and through the double doors. As she ambled toward the restroom, she saw rooms named Venus, Marduk, Mars, Macha, and Min. On the door of Min was an Egyptian god holding a flail in one hand and possessing an erect penis.

These must be the rooms.

The door to Kokopelli opened and a stunning thirty-something man with unruly blonde surfer hair emerged carrying what looked to be a specimen. Lilly averted her gaze to protect his privacy and anonymity.

"Hey," said the guy from Kokopelli with a wide, gleaming smile.

Lilly almost lost her footing. A man, who just minutes before was donating, was now being sociable. He noticed that she was looking at the sign on the door.

"Kokopelli. I named this door. He is a fertility deity depicted as a humpbacked flute player. Native Americans

9

believed that his penis was detachable, and he sometimes left it in a river in order to have sex with girls who bathed there."

Lilly laughed, but it snuck out as a giggle. *Oh, god.* "I'm looking for the restroom." Lilly wanted to make sure he knew her visit to this hallway of fertility gods and goddesses had a non-reproductive purpose—that she wasn't a desperate woman seeking his or anyone else's sperm.

"Oh, it's down there." He pointed in the direction she was headed. "It's the last door after Ishtar—the goddess of love and maiming. Go figure." He let out a belly laugh before he and his specimen disappeared around the corner.

On her way back from the restroom, Lilly noticed that the Marduk door was open. She peered in and saw huge, round silver storage tanks, storing, no doubt, millions of sperm. So, these weren't the donor rooms after all.

Lilly still wanted to sneak a peek at Donor Hall, so she went straight for the double doors. The donation rooms were not named. They were painted red, orange, green, and blue. The door to the red room was open, so she stepped inside. She only noticed a curtained closet before she heard footsteps. Lilly heard a reproductive counselor directing a donor to the Green Room. Each door had a light hanging over it. Only the light over the blue door was illuminated. Lilly imagined the scene inside and quickly headed back to

Bridget's office. She didn't want to catch a guy right after the act.

"Did you get lost in Spermatozoa Hall? Some of our staff members clearly don't have enough to do, so they name the doors," Bridget said.

Lilly laughed, and then wondered how she might broach the topic of the blonde Kokopelli. "Um, so there was this guy who came out of Kokopelli, and I was wondering if I might...well...be able to consider his..."

"Sperm?"

"Yeah, how might I find out about him?"

"If he was coming out of Kokopelli, he was a donor technician. It doesn't work like that, Lilly. You must select an anonymous donor."

"But I can't tell much about the donors without photos. It's just that I'm picking a complete stranger to be the father of my child."

"That's the strength and the weakness of the modern sperm bank, Lilly. Anonymity is what most people are going for. It's much less complicated, I can assure you." Bridget turned in her chair and squinted at the invasive sunbeam making its way across her desk. "Most people in this city whip themselves into a sun-worshipping frenzy when the sun makes it grand entrance, but I prefer the cool grey drizzle." Bridget leaned forward to let Lilly in on her secret. "Don't tell anyone." She turned around and pulled the curtains with a drawstring to keep out the mid-day sun.

It was then that Lilly concocted a plan.

Lilly took her basal temperature religiously until she knew she was ovulating. Then she donned a brunette Parisian page-boy wig, Jackie-O glasses, and a silk scarf tied beneath her chin. She wore a trench coat and black patent leather go-go boots. When she got off the elevator to the sperm bank, she headed toward Donor Hall. All of the red lights above the rooms were on except for the middle room. Before entering, she made sure the coast was clear.

The room was dark and windowless with a leather couch, a TV, a closet with a curtain, and a bathroom area. There were stacks of magazines, porn movies, and white cotton towels. She slipped in behind the curtain and waited. Her heart beat vigorously under her coat.

At 10:15 am, she heard footsteps and then the door creak open. The counselor delivered the donation instructions in a bland, monotone voice. Then she said, "Here's your stack of girlie mags to help with production. Questions?" Lilly couldn't hear the question, but the answer was, "Boy mags?" Then the shuffling and sorting of magazines. "Here, you go. OK, good luck."

Good luck? Did people need luck for this process? Lilly wondered behind the curtain. After the counselor left, she risked a peek. The guy, a short and nerdy accountant-type, was leafing through magazines. After determining that he wasn't to be her donor, she just listened. The page-turning stopped and then silence followed. Apparently, he had selected a fantasy boy. The accountant moaned in deep tones. The tones worked their way up the scale until they sounded like the moans of a woman. When Lilly thought the moans couldn't get any higher, he hit a high C and then said, "Lockheed, oh Lockheed, launch me."

A soprano accountant with missile-launching fantasies was not going to be the father of her child.

The Lockheed-lover was followed by a mullet-wearing rock-n-roller, a comb-over Russian, a pudgy gnome, a surly Indian, and a quiet Asian-American who donated without a sound. After all the grunting, moaning, and groaning, Lilly was beginning to have ejaculation fatigue and thinking that for her plan to work, she'd have to be Jackie-O behind the curtain for weeks, maybe months.

The door opened and someone came in without the counselor and her bland ejaculating-into-a-cup instructions. *Strange*, Lilly thought. The person rearranged the furniture and then sat. She snuck a peek; it was Kokopelli, the beautiful blonde surfer. He was reading a book titled *Internal Ejaculation*.

She moved back behind the curtain, her heart racing and her mind whirring. *What was he doing here? It could only be one thing. Could I? Would I?*

She hadn't really thought past the camouflage and the curtain. Her face flushed and her palms got clammy. *It's now or never!* She emerged from behind the curtain.

"Hi there." She couldn't think of what else to say.

Kokopelli's unruly hair rearranged itself as he nearly lost his balance on the table that served as his meditation platform. "Shit! You scared me! Are you a voyeur or a spy?"

"Both, I guess. I'm a spy on a mission to find the perfect sperm."

"Man, good luck with that." He set *Internal Ejaculation* face down.

"I think I've found it."

"Cool. Yeah, we have thousands of specimens in our tanks. Our counselors are top notch at helping people find what they're looking for."

"I don't think you understand."

"Don't understand what?"

"Aren't you here to donate?"

"Well, yeah. You want to watch or something? Kinky!"

"No, no, that's not what I'm saying."

"You want me to give you my specimen? That would be premeditated sperm stealing, and I would be an accomplice. I think you can get 15 to life for that." He smirked and leaned back on his hands.

"What I'm asking is if you would be willing to donate directly."

He laughed, thinking it was a joke. But she didn't crack a smile.

"Seriously?"

"Dead serious."

"Man, I don't know what to say. This is highly unexpected." He looked down at his feet, sighed, and put his hand to his forehead.

Lilly's heart sank as she braced herself for a rejection.

Then he looked Lilly straight in the eye and said, "But, hell, I'm all for cutting out the middle man."

As soon as Lilly got the go-ahead, she acted quickly for fear that he would change his mind. The scene looked like a fast motion striptease act. She pulled off her coat, scarf, dress, and panties and threw them down on the chair. He hesitated, not sure what to do next. Then he jumped down from the table and took her by the waist. He helped her onto the table and laid her down.

"Dude, I can't believe I'm doing this. I hope nobody looks for today's specimen, because they ain't gonna find it."

To Lilly, this experience was better than any pointed turkey baster or prodding medical procedure with frozen sperm. It was a direct deposit.

Needle Man Sticks Bat Girl

I first went to him to cure general malaise. It had crept in and was my constant companion. The permanent expression on my face was a blank but startled: is this all there is? Everyone was always asking me, "What's wrong?"

And I would lie. "Nothing, really."

But after all my schooling—I had earned a Ph.D. in bats—I was stuck in a cubicle writing copy for a natural history museum. My current gig was writing for *Body Worlds*. Stuff like, *Come see dead people. Dead Germans frozen in time, in action. Slices of humans. The work of a cannibal, serial killer.* But of course I couldn't write what I really thought about the dead people exhibit. So, instead I wrote: *Experience the power and vulnerability of the wondrous human body. A once-in-a-lifetime chance to explore what's on the inside.*

I originally considered med school, but I couldn't get past the idea of working with dead people injected with formaldehyde. As it turned out, the cadavers found me. Don't ever run away from anything in life; it will always find you.

Everyone assured me I was lucky to have such a cool job. I would respond with a grateful-for-my-cool-job smirk, but I didn't feel anything. Not grateful. Not ungrateful. Just nothing.

People at work got creeped out by the bat décor in my cubicle. I had a plastic bat on a bouncing string hanging from above. My coworkers sometimes bumped into it and squealed. I had bats velcroed to my beige cubicle walls. I hung a giant bat poster with dozens of different species displayed, which would usually get an "eeew" or an "eek" from women before they turned their backs on it. I was alien to my gender—one that was squeamish with all things creepy-crawly.

This was as close as I could come to having a bat cave in my current life. Sometimes I imagined that if I were living with bats, I'd be more alive. But it was hard to find bat cave jobs, unless one were an animated character in Gotham City. Which I'm not, unfortunately.

So, when he first asked me why I had come, I said, "I feel nothing."

"Nothing, Sydney?"

"Nothing."

"Surely you feel something."

"No, surely I don't."

"That doesn't give me much to go on."

"Do I have to give you something to go on?"

"It would help. Mostly people come to me because they feel too much."

I laughed. "Wouldn't that be nice?"

"Your laugh lights up the room. That's how I know you feel something."

His comment caught me by surprise. It sounded more like a pick-up line than an Eastern medicine observation, but what did I know? "Really? I do?"

He scribbled something in his notes. He made a little table and wrote things in it. I tried to read upside down. But it was squiggles and signs. I wondered if he even knew what he was writing.

He lifted his pen to his mouth, gazed into my eyes with his translucent blues offset by thick eyelashes. His eyes looked like oasis pools, or at least what I imagined such pools to look like. I felt uneasy with him peering into my world, such as it was. I focused on the sputtering fountain to break the intensity.

"Anything else to report?"

I wanted to tell him that I was sick of writing upbeat copy about dead people and that I preferred bats to humans, but I decided not to open with that. "Guess not."

"Do you really mean that?" He touched my arm.

"It's just that…Yes, I mean that."

"OK, up on the table." He directed me to the table near the window with bamboo shades retracted to just above eye level. The room was sparsely furnished as if a Zen interior decorator who subscribed to "less is more" had designed it. There was exactly one desk, an acupuncture table covered by a jasmine-splashed sheet, a chest, a bamboo plant, and a fountain next to his desk. The fountain didn't so much flow as gurgle like a draining sink.

"Lie down and I'll get your pulses."

My pulses. The thing that differentiated me from the dead people in the exhibit. Otherwise, that might be me posed on a skateboard or in a tutu, my muscles, ligaments, and tendons exposed for eternity.

He held my left hand for a few minutes and then walked around and held my right. His hands were calloused and warm. Then he circled back around and held my left hand and then my right. It was like when someone holds your hand when you're grieving or something. It made me want to cry.

At one point, he said, "Hmm."

"What?"

"The gate to your courtyard is closed and the metal and wood are out of balance. You're a fire person."

Huh? It sounded like a bad horoscope. "I didn't know I had a courtyard."

"We all have courtyards."

"Maybe my courtyard is on fire."

"Your pulses are bow-string."

He didn't acknowledge my acu-humor. He closed his eyes and held my hand some more.

"Like a violin?" If I were a string instrument, I'd be more like a cello.

He walked over to his book, put his hand on his chin, scratched his curly, blond hair and then walked over to the needle zone.

Oh, god. Puncturing time. I wasn't one of those fainting at the sight of needles people, but I can't say I was at peace with them, either. Not like I was about bats.

He said, "Shirt off. I need your back."

"You do? But I don't have a bra on."

"That's OK."

OK with whom? "Do you have a blanket or something?"

He grabbed a blanket from inside the chest.

Like you could have offered me one. Were you trying to sneak a peek? I slipped off my shirt and held the blanket tightly over my chest.

He touched my back up and down my spine, counting aloud.

"Now breathe."

I complied, trying not to tense. The needle slid in and caused a reverberating sensation. Not good. Not bad.

"Release."

We did the breathe-and-release thing half a dozen times, each needle feeling different—hot, stinging, rippling pain, electrifying, pinching. Who knew there were so many different sensations when punctured?

"You can put your shirt back on. Then I need your pulses again."

He poked me with needles in my feet, hands, and fingers, until I felt as if I were a pin cushion.

It was after feeling like a pin cushion that I started to notice a change. I looked up from a supine position into the brilliant blue eyes of this fair-haired Needle Man. I hadn't seen him when I walked in, but I sure noticed him as I walked out.

The needle bearer permeated my daily thoughts. I thought about him biking to work with a latte in my water bottle holder. I thought about him while crafting bullet points about dead people laminated for public viewing. He popped into my mind while searching the internet for bat jobs. Bat Girl stuck on Needle Man, or rather Needle Man sticks Bat Girl.

I still couldn't feel anything about my life—only about him. I found myself counting the days until my next session. Five, four, three, two, one.

"Did you notice anything different this week?"

"Not really." I lied.

"OK, we'll have to do something about that. Won't we?" His eyes locked on mine, as though he was trying to unlock a clue. "Up on the table." He grasped my hand with both hands and closed his eyes. I looked up at him. He bit his lip in concentration. His eyebrows collided and his nostrils flared. He looked as though he sensed me—the unfeeling one. I felt a twinge of vulnerability and shifted my weight. I felt antsy. I suddenly didn't want to be seen.

"We need to clear your heart so your spirit can have a home."

"My spirit doesn't have a home? That sounds serious."

"It is. Like all gates, the Spirit Gate must open and close freely. The spirit must be able to move freely, responding to any need. Locked out of its home, or with the gate stuck open, the spirit cannot rest."

"That makes sense, I suppose. My spirit doesn't have a home."

He took my wrist and stuck a needle in my wrist-fold.

"Ouch!" It smarted like a funny-bone incident.

"Good."

"Good?"

"That was your triple-heater point. It had a major release."

"What does that mean?"

"I can't really explain it in layman's terms."

"Try."

"The ch'i from your wind is hollow."

"Oh, I see what you mean." I had no idea what that meant but the hollowness seemed fitting. Yours truly, a hollow shell of a human.

He slid his hand along my upper arm; his touch tingled throughout my body, as though his hand itself was an instrument of acupuncture.

"I need to do a head point."

"You're going to stick a needle in my head?"

"The archway to the heavenly temple is blocked; your spirit can't get in."

I thought about the plight of my wandering spirit and agreed to the head needle. "OK." The head needle went in and a warm feeling washed over my body that energized me. "Wow."

"Did you feel that, too?" He rubbed my back and said, "Lie back." He put his hands under my head, neck, back, and then head again. He touched my head, cradling it in his hands, like a giant delicate bird egg. I imagined a mama bird treasuring her baby bird, waiting for a chick to emerge. I felt a warm tear inching down my cheek. I reached up to intercept it. His hand met mine.

"Don't stop it." His words opened a floodgate. Tears streamed down my cheeks; I let them fall. I had no idea why I was crying. He shifted his hands to the top of my head and stroked my hair. I wondered if it was appropriate clinician behavior, but I didn't care.

He waited until the tears stopped and said, "I think your spirit found its home."

"How can you be sure?"

"I need your pulses again." He finished stroking my hair and got up to do his usual hand-holding routine. He smiled down at me. "Perfect. You're all set."

But I didn't want to be all set. I wanted to stay and be needled. *Needled more? What was going on?*

I slouched at the end of a long, rectangular conference table at work, listening to meeting attendees talk in soundbites about pitching dead people to the living.

"How can we de-emphasize the cadaver factor?" asked the PR director.

25

"Focus on the mysteries of the human body and the ability for the first time in history to view the magic of life," said a PR associate with hair that curled up and under and magenta lips lined outside her actual lips. A little too clowny for cadaver talk.

My mind trailed off to Needle Man—the tufts of hair on his pink scalp, his liquid blue eyes, mouth in a permanent question: Where are you, Sydney? His tender touch and electrifying needles. His ability to see through me—as though my body was transparent.

"Sydney, what's your take on this approach? You've got to be comfortable writing this copy."

I was startled back into the room when I heard my name. "I'm sorry I was thinking about another aspect of the project; can you repeat what you said?"

"I said our pitch should emphasize the magic and mysteries of the human body." All eyes were on me.

"I don't know. To me, there's no magic in body slices. I think we need to say it like it is. The specimens are without skin so you can see the bones, muscles, tendons, nerves, blood vessels, organs, even genitals. See-through people." The minute I closed my mouth, I was horrified by my honesty. It would never fly with this bunch. I would now have to back-peddle somehow.

A hush overtook the room. Eyes darted about; people shifted in their seats and cleared their throats. I readied myself to take back what I said, but as I opened my mouth to rescind, the PR director said, "You know, Sydney, I think you're on to something. Your approach has a two-fold benefit. One is that people will know what they're getting into. The second is that people will be fascinated by guts and truth."

Guts and truth. Leave it to the PR director to come up with a compelling soundbite about dead people.

After the guts and truth bit, and me turning into the meeting rock star, I checked my daytimer, not for my next dead person deadline, but for my next appointment with Needle Man. Four days. I felt my stomach flip-flop thinking about Thursday. It would be four days of writing cadaver copy before I would feel the electricity again. I wondered what was happening to me. *Was this healing or something else?*

"Did you notice anything different this week?"

"Not really." I lied again.

Needle Man's face dropped and he spot-checked his file, searching for something in his notes.

"Well, I suppose I do feel something."

"Really?" He glanced up quickly, leaned forward, and said, "Tell me more."

"I'm feeling more alive than dead."

"That's fantastic. There's more you're not telling me."

"That could be true of anyone."

"Sydney, stop evading. There's something you need to tell me."

"How is it that you can see me so clearly?" I asked him. *Oh shit! That came out wrong. I'm revealing too much.*

"Your soul is like a glass lake."

"But I thought my spirit was homeless." *Good. Sufficiently snarky.*

"Sydney, your spirit is magnificent."

I felt suddenly exposed; as though I was standing naked in front of Needle Man.

He motioned for me to get on the table in my usual supine position. He then slipped his hand down my shirt, in between my breasts. I flinched. His hand swiped my nipple.

What was he doing? I almost said something, but then figured it was an unintended swipe. But part of me hoped it wasn't. He removed his hand and slipped it down the top of my pants to the edge of my pubic hair. Again, I nearly said something, but I felt a pulsing sensation between my legs. I wanted him to touch me.

I was lying on a clinical table, wanting this needle-bearing man to make love to me. *Jesus.*

His treatment went longer than usual—shirt off, shirt on, lying down, and sitting up, turning around, needles in back, needles in arm, feet, and hands. I felt thoroughly punctured. His last point was the Heart Protector, which isn't what it sounds like. He told me it protects your heart so you can love freely. It sent shockwaves through my system. I felt like an overflowing stream of passion.

Was this acupuncture or was it voodoo?

I decided to investigate. I got online and googled "acupuncture + love spells." I came across this: "There are meridians and acupoints that if simulated can trigger an outpouring of love. If the ch'i has been stagnant for a time, the patient can be vulnerable to those around her, especially to the practitioner, who is opening up the heart channels."

As I researched, I realized that this man, this love voodoo doctor, was intentionally making me fall in love with him.

I planned to show up at my next appointment wearing a leotard that had to be removed in order for him to get to points on my back. I envisioned slipping off my leotard to reveal my lacy thong and bra. He would be so taken with my breasts, my pierced belly, my tattooed derriere, he would tell me to lie back and close my eyes. He would climb on top of me and reach a point deep inside me, where no needle had gone before.

"Hi Sydney," he said with a sparkle in his eye.

Or did I just imagine that? "Hi," I said trying to hold back a mischievous grin.

"What's so funny?" He poked me in the tummy.

"Nothing. I'm just happy to see you."

"What's new in the world of Sydney?"

"I'm feeling so much; it's overwhelming."

"Good, good," he jotted this down in his notes. "I'm so glad to hear it. Jump up on the table for me. Let's feel those pulses."

You'll be feeling my pulses in no time. I laid back and gave him my hand. A bolt of electricity traveled between our hands.

"OK, I'm going to do some feet and hand points."

"You don't need my back today?"

"Nope. Why? Did you want me to do your back?" he asked in a teasing tone.

"Well, if you don't need to, it's OK." I looked away to conceal my disappointment.

He inserted several needles in my feet—in and out. Then he took my pulses again. He went to the head of the table, and put his hands under my back and neck. Next thing I knew, his hand was on top of my leotard—in between my breasts.

This is where I come in. I took his hand in mine and moved it over to my breast. Then I held my hand on top of his to signal that I wanted him there on my erect nipple.

"What are you doing?" He withdrew his hand.

"Isn't it what you want?"

"No, not at all. Sydney, Sydney, Sydney. I'm just feeling your core body temperature."

"Oh, c'mon love voodoo doc. We've come this far." I couldn't believe I was saying this. My boldness was even a surprise to me.

"Love voodoo doc? Holy shit, you have the wrong idea!"

"Don't tell me you haven't been using your needles to get me to fall in love with you. It's OK; I won't tell, if you don't." I struck a pouty smile.

He went over to his chair and sunk into it facing his desk, resting his head in his hands. I sat up and swung my legs around on the table and crossed them, sex-kitten style. "I won't file a sexual harassment suit. You have my word."

"I don't know where you got this love voodoo stuff."

31

I had a dizzy spell—the room was spinning and closing in on me. Had I imagined everything? Didn't he love my laugh? Couldn't he see my spirit? He helped my spirit find a home; he could see me like no other man had ever seen me.

"It's OK. Here, here's your shirt." He held my shirt up as I slid my arms into the sleeves. "Now that you're emotionally thawing, it's not unusual to attach to the healer helping you to feel again. It's completely normal."

His textbook words stung me like dozens of needles inserted into my heart at once, obliterating the Heart Protector he once sought to protect. I hid behind my hands and sobbed. I wanted him to say my spirit's home was with him. I wanted to hear that my laugh ignited his passion. I wanted him to cradle my head in his hands.

Instead he handed me a Kleenex box and asked if I had anything else to share to gain closure.

Oh, god, not the C-word. "Will you keep seeing me?" I already knew the answer, but I needed to hear it from him.

"I think it's best if we find you someone else."

"But your job is only half-finished."

"I'll refer you to someone just as capable who can take it from where I left off. You'll be in good hands."

I was back in my cube, writing copy and stuck on: *You'll never look at the human body the same way again.*

I couldn't think clearly. The Needle Man incident hung heavily on my heart. My heart had opened up. I felt, and then the door slammed shut.

The phone rang. I answered in monotone, "PR department, Sydney." It was the Director from Oregon State University that I had interviewed with months ago. She was offering me a position as a bat research technician in southeast Alaska. She reminded me that the duties would include capturing and handling bats, guano collection, and recording and analyzing echolocation calls.

She rattled off question after question, gauging my enthusiasm to perform field work throughout the night in rugged, potentially uncomfortable settings (bugs, weather, darkness, etc.). She told me that bear activity would be high in most study areas and I would be required to carry and be prepared to use a high-powered rifle.

Beige cubicles, laminated dead people, and cuckoo voodoo docs versus bugs, bats, and bears. "Are you kidding me?"

"Of course, you'll want time to think it over."

"I'm in."

The last thing I did before I and my giant backpack and duffel bag left for Alaska was to call Needle Man. I wanted to show him that I was moving on. If I had stopped to think about it, the call was for my sake, not his. He had probably filed it neatly under "client transference."

"Hello?"

"Hi. It's Sydney."

"Oh, hello." He sounded halting, tentative.

"I just wanted you to know that I'm headed to Alaska to work with bats."

"Good for you. Listen, I'm sorry about the misunderstanding. But I knew once your spirit was in the temple, you'd find your path."

"Yeah, thanks." He was right about one thing; my spirit had come home.

He was wrong about my home, though. It wasn't a courtyard or a temple. It was a bat cave.

Chairs in Air

In a fit of fury, Charlie pulled off her tattered, paint-splotched overalls and unbraided her hair. She couldn't be bothered to wear anything other than overalls. She forced her blonde wavy hair into an up-do that would embarrass Jacoby, her self-appointed style consultant and agent, and threw on a short black dress and black ballerina slippers. People expected or at least weren't shocked when artists were nonplussed, anarchic, and chaotic.

As she stood in front of her vanity, pulling spirally wisps out of her up-do, she thought about how much she despised gala openings. The posers, critics, artist wannabes and minor celebs came out in droves to see and be seen with her work as a backdrop to the drama of their lives. Mostly, people were looking for cultured people to sleep with. Why, she didn't know. In her experience, cultured people made the worst lovers. Give her a truck driver, Harley guy, carpenter, fire fighter, or cop any day. The glasses gave it away. The more self-conscious the glasses frames, the worse the sexual experience. Too many colors and the guy was a premature ejaculator. Retro classic and the man couldn't get it up. Rimless and the owner was pasty, doughy, and a lazy lover. Preppy and just one position worked for him—doggy style. The only glasses that indicated sexual promise were the *whatever-I'll-take-those* frames. That guy was too engrossed in life to care what framed his eyes. He was looking out on the world, not in on himself.

It was a convenient screening system that Charlie had never revealed to anyone. And in Manhattan, it eliminated almost everyone, which was why she was still single. In her version of a glasses-frame universe, the entire island of Manhattan was either climaxing too quickly, malfunctioning, lazily getting off, or stuck in a sexual rut.

The thing Charlie dreaded the most about openings was having to explain and dissect her art, searching for psycho-socio-cultural-anthropological underpinnings and themes that didn't exist. She could never say, "I have no fucking idea why I created a five-story chair out of discarded chairs." But that was the truth. She had no fucking idea why. Before these things, she fantasized about running through the crowd with their precious Merlots and mini-crudités, screaming, "This piece is artistic purging. It's nothing more than psychic vomit."

But instead she said things like, "The refrigerators used in *Refrigerator Art* symbolize our inability to truly feed ourselves. This probably makes you feel empty, hungry for something more—right? Refrigerators store our food. They're central to our lives, yet we abandon them when they no longer serve us. Just like our souls."

Sipping Merlot and staining her carefully bleached teeth, the Every Woman Art Connoisseur nodded and said, "Mmm-mm, yes, yes, I see. Brilliant." But she never really saw.

Charlie had waited until the last minute to come up with her faux-artistic interpretation of *Chairs in Air*. As she rode the subway to Central Park, she would conjure up some deconstructionist drivel. The subway was an urban Petri dish for intellectual masturbatory diatribes.

As Charlie hung onto the train's safety railing and stared blankly at the concrete tunnel rushing past, she rehearsed, "I developed a deconstructivist form of historical narrative through which we might engage critically with questions of ethico-cultural value. The chair, you see, is the gateway to civilization. By elevating the chairs and stacking them one upon another, I articulate the building blocks of civilization."

The only problem with initiating this conversation was if someone continued the dialogue, she would have nothing more to add. "Off to mingle," she'd say as she offered a pairing of I'm-the-busy-and-important-artist smile and shrug.

The other thing that helped her get through these bug-in-a-jar experiences was to drink just a little too much. If she became visibly drunk, her funding sources would malign her and refuse to fund future installations. So, tipsy was her goal.

Her phone rang. It was her agent, a nervous twit of a man with frameless glasses, worrying that she had forgotten about the opening.

"Of course I didn't forget, Jacoby. What do you take me for—a twit? I know I may have done twitty things in the past, but I'm past twit now."

He told her that twitty wasn't a word, and missing her earlier *Blender Bender* installation was inexcusable.

"Oh for God's sake, Jacoby, haven't we gotten past *Blender Bender*? I'll be there in…" She looked at her watch. The opening had already started. "…five minutes." It was a lie, but she didn't want the wimpy wrath of Jacoby. Give her full-strength wrath any day; feeble wrath made her cringe.

Jacoby squealed and said she'd better make it snappy or the NEA would pull. That's what he always said to scare her.

She was starting to see the NEA as an artistic Third Reich.

The attendees were milling about the base of *Chairs in Air*. They looked like inconsequential devotees worshipping the mighty God of Chairs. And if the God came tumbling down—chair by chair—the followers would be smashed in the act of devotion. To ensure the stability of the installation, the NEA required an inspection with a mountain of documents for everyone to sign. Art as bureaucracy.

Like a heat-seeking missile, Jacoby spotted her the minute she set foot in the area. He was looking grim and disappointed. "I don't have words to describe how wrong this is." He whisked her over to the NEAers in chic suits and rectangular glasses. "She's here!" In an instant, he had gone from grim to gay, which he was, and ass-kicking to ass-licking, which he did.

"Ah-ha, our artiste des chaises!" said Bibi, the female NEAer in an owning class kind of way, daintily offering her hand followed by two air kisses. Charlie availed her cheeks and then dipped in a faux curtsy. "It's going smashingly, Charlotte! Ah, but you need some bubbly." Bibi snapped her fingers in the air and magically a caterer appeared with a tray of flutes. Charlie didn't wait for the caterer to pluck a flute from the tray; she helped herself to not one but two glasses of bubbly.

"Ha ha, Charlotte," said Jacoby. "Silly girl, you needn't have gotten one for me."

"I didn't." Charlie threw her head back, downing the champagne in one gulp, and putting the empty glass on the tray. "It's for me."

"Silly girl," Jacoby said again, offering eye contact as an apology to all the NEAers who were nursing their own bubbly flutes. "Charlotte is so grateful for your support without which this wouldn't have been possible. Right Charlotte? I propose a toast." Jacoby lifted his glass to *Chairs in Air.*

Charlie nodded mid-swig, pretending to see someone important off in the distance. "If you'll excuse me."

Jacoby trailed, giving her an earful about her childish behavior toward the NEA.

She approached a guy with wild auburn locks, a soul patch, and glasses atop his head. Damn! She couldn't make a quick on-the-spot assessment. She grabbed him by the arm and said, "Pretend we're having a deeply personal conversation."

"Um, OK." She pulled him closer and although his eyes were conveying "*crazy*," his body obeyed.

"Jacoby, not a good time," she said as she waved him away behind her back. Jacoby kept moving but admonished her with his eyes.

"Sorry, um…"

"Noah."

"Sorry, Noah. Charlie. I'm running…"

"From the law?"

"Oh, no, nothing like that. Running from my agent and the NEA."

"That's a new one. Most people would kill to have the NEA pursuing them. Why?"

"Oh, I'm the artist and they funded this and I was going to have to explain myself, my art, my reason for being, and infuse meaning into their luxuriously dull lives. Frankly, I'm not in the mood. I need more champagne." Charlie snapped her fingers, but no one came. How was it that even the caterers knew the guest list? Clearly they knew she was one of them.

Noah chuckled. "Maybe it would be faster if I went to fetch some for us."

"OK, but don't leave me alone for long, pleeease." Just as Noah left, a flute tray floated by. Charlie took two glasses and downed them both in a few seconds flat.

"That bad, huh?" said the flute carrier.

"You have no idea," said Charlie. With that, she realized that she had gone past tipsy. Her *Chairs in Air* had become a living, breathing entity, swaying against the Manhattan skyline. Or was it she who was swaying?

A whimsical, wispy, willowy woman approached Charlie with her finger in the air, looking as if she were testing the wind for sailing. "You must be the artist."

"Yes, that's me!" Charlie steadied herself and prepared for a long-winded discourse on the evolution of found objects as art.

"I just had to find you and tell you what an absolute waste of time and money I think this project is. It's an eyesore to have a mountain, no—a heap of trashy chairs littering Central Park. To call this art is abominable, simply an outrage. In all my years as an art collector and connoisseur, I've never seen anything so offensive to the Manhattan cityscape. Never, ever! If I could, I would supervise the dismantling of this debacle at once."

"And your name is?"

"Sari."

"Listen, Sarah…"

"Sari."

"As in the Indian dress, sari?"

"No, as in how I feel about coming to this event."

"You're entitled to your opinion, of course. But don't you see that these chairs are a de…" Charlie hiccupped. "…constructivist form of historical narrative through which we might engage critically with questions of ethico-cultural value?" Hiccup. "The chair, you see, is the g-g-g…" Hiccup.

"...gateway to civilization. By elevating the chairs and stacking them one upon another, I art..." Hiccup. "...iculate the building blocks of civilization." The hiccups were coming fast and furiously now.

Noah showed up balancing three glasses of champagne with two hands after she delivered her rehearsed art-o-babble. If she had been sober, she would have recognized that the hiccups rendered her speech ineffectual.

A bony pointed finger came at Charlie. Trying to focus on it made her cross-eyed and dizzy.

"You have no idea what this is or why you created it. Further, you have no reason to believe anyone will care or understand why it's taking up space. It's not art. Art is a thing of beauty or intrigue that prompts one to see the world differently through a new set of eyes. It opens up dimensions not previously accessible. This is a pile of rubbish pure and simple," spouted Sari. She took her bony finger back.

Although Charlie put on an act of detached toughness, this acerbic diatribe cut into her like a figurative sculptor's knife in wet clay, preparing to extract her heart and soul. Before the surgical removal was carried out, she reached over, grabbed a glass of champagne from Noah and threw it into Sari's face.

Sari froze between flight and fight. Then grimly, she added, "I'll see to it that you never exhibit in this city again."

Glancing at her program, she finished, "Charlotte Bertrand." And arranging her hair and face, she dramatically peered up at *Chairs in Air*, glared at Charlie, shook her head in disgust and stormed off in her dainty summer flats.

"You wasted a good glass of champagne," said Noah in an attempt at levity.

Charlie was trembling and tears streamed down her stoic face. Noah offered her a glass of champagne.

She shook her head. "I can't hold my liquor. I should have never started. It's just that I hate these things, but attendance is required as part of the legal stipulations of the contract. The undersigned must be in attendance at the opening of the aforementioned exhibit to field questions about the artistic process, media, and significance of the piece as a contribution to modern art. Blah, blah, blah."

"Hey, don't be hard on yourself. That stuff hurts. Really hurts."

She looked up at him through wet lashes, nodding, and said, "You know?"

"God, yes. Hurts to the core." And placed his fist on his heart.

Wow. A man who knows where his heart is. "You are an artist, too?"

"Nope, eco-warrior. But we get our share of impassioned protesters."

44

"Oh, a save-the-Earth guy."

"Yep."

"Have you done it yet?"

"God, no. Long way to go, if ever."

"Do you live in trees slated for deforestation, stand between baby seals and hunters, and steer dinghies into the nets of whaling ships? That kind of stuff?"

"Something like that. Listen, I think your *Chairs* are brilliant—a genius improvisation, amalgamation, and compilation of the downfall of society."

Charlie laughed. "You got that out of this?" She pointed up at the sculpture. "Chairs are the downfall of society?" She erupted in laughter.

"You bet! Not only do they promote stagnation and vegetation, they also kill the imagination."

"You're really into the 'tions.' Aren't you?"

"Not at all my intention." Although they both knew it was cheap entertainment, they laughed anyway.

"Hey, listen, I want to show you something," Charlie said, moving away from the milling crowd.

"Can Madame Artiste leave the premises?"

"The artiste has done enough damage for one opening. Don't you think?" She grabbed him by the arm and guided him over to a stand of trees that hid the world from view. Then she pulled his head to hers and kissed him deeply, her tongue playing with his lips, tongue, and mouth. A surge swept from her heart to her pelvis and she plunged her hand into his pants, not having to search for his penis, standing hard and hot.

"But Charlie..."

"Doesn't matter." She elevated her leg to open herself up for him. He unzipped and plunged deeply into her, not off-balance by the awkwardness of the standing pose. They bent their knees slightly as they thrust to meet the other. Her moans were muffled and low, but as he grew stiffer and their pace quickened, her moaning crescendoed and danced around the scale. She tilted and rotated her pelvis in such a way that made his climactic moan upstage hers. She dropped her leg as if nothing had happened and kissed him quickly. He looked like he didn't know what had hit him.

"Eco-boy, I needed that," she cried out as she pulled him back toward the opening. He was hastily tucking and buckling and straightening.

"Shit. I have no idea what that was. I'm not complaining. But I have no idea what that was."

She leaned over, nibbled his ear, and whispered, "Eco-boy just got laid. Now let me see your glasses," she said as she pulled them over his eyes.

The *whatever-I'll-take-those* frames.

The Sweetness of Salt

Alexis didn't peer over her muted cubicle wall when she called out, "Hey Jen, got another word for throbbing?"

Without missing a beat, Jen replied, "Engorged."

"C'mon, is that the best you can do?" Alexis had hoped Jen could offer a little inspiration for her erotica slump.

"Sorry, I've shot my wad today. I had to churn out a ménage-a-trois scene with swingers."

"Better you than me."

"Yeah, I knew I was in trouble when at our last staff meeting, Sylvaine was talking about the upsurge in swinging among average American couples. I was thinking—oh, god, please don't give me swingers. And, lo and behold, I got an email the next day with my new assignment—"The Girl *and* Boy Next Door.""

"Count yourself lucky. My next assignment is paranormal erotica."

Jen's head popped up. Her strawberry blonde ringlets were going haywire. "Oh my god. What is that—alien porn?"

"Who the fuck knows? This genre-merging is hard to keep up with. So, engorged is as good as it gets?" Alexis shoved her art-house rectangular glasses to the top of her head to serve as a headband. Her purple jet-black hair was always falling in her eyes.

"Why don't you refer to your arousing adjectives handout from the Latin love bug?" A paper fan appeared above the cubicle wall. Jen hid her face behind it—geisha style—and then fanned herself. "Is it getting hot in here or is it just me?" Jen let out a belly-laugh and plunked down. The great cubicle disappearing act.

"Guess I'll have to consult Guillermo's list. This is due to copyediting by the end of the week. I've got three more sex scenes—BJ in a saloon, rear entry on a horse, and vanilla in hay."

"Your protag is doing a horse? Riding Queen Catherine style. Ouch! What genre is that? Beastiromantica? Hey, if you need help with the BJ scene, remember, I'm the BJ scene queen."

"May I ask if you're drawing from your own…?"

"No, you may not." Jen laughed.

Feeling at a loss for penis descriptors, Alexis leaned back and chewed the tip of the penis eraser atop her pen, which read: Romantica Fest 2018: Romantica writers do it with the lights on. Each year, thousands of romantica (romance + erotica) writers, seeking inspired ways to write about sex, descended upon Manhattan. They attended sessions, such as Between the Sheets, Not Your Average Bedtime Stories, and Steaming the Windows and Other Special Effects. Her all-time favorite session was given by a sizzling hot Venezuelan man named Guillermo called Arousing Adjectives. Guillermo had dark, curly hair swept back by designer shades, revealing bright green, almond-shaped eyes offset by dark skin. His dimples were parentheses setting off his cocky smile and overly-bleached white teeth. As he described the power of adjectives in sex scenes, Alexis guessed that the entire conference room of at least fifty women and three men (few men braved the halls of Romantica Fest) were applying the adjectives to their fantasies about Guillermo. She wondered if the conference organizers didn't select him on purpose so they would all have a take-away—eye candy for the mind and pen.

At another session, she had learned 101 words for penis, 55 words for vagina, and 35 words for intercourse. "Flesh kabob" was the ringer for penis and "furburger" took the prize for vagina. Once, when trying to practice her vocabulary, she invited a nerdy literary guy to put his flesh kabob in her furburger. This invitation promptly ended her internet date, which is exactly what she was going for. It worked so well for Alexis, some of her friends tried it; however, most of them had takers. One of her friend's dates left off the "fur" while talking dirty, and she asked if he wanted fries with that. He didn't get it. This didn't help Alexis' sinking opinion of the modern American man.

Because of her profession, Alexis had become her friends' and family's clearinghouse for all things erotic and romantic. When friends wanted to write love letters, she co-authored; when guys planned to propose, she collaborated (read: composed the proposal); when girlfriends wanted to spice up their sex lives, they called her to get ideas for accessorizing and positioning.

As Alexis studied Guillermo's list in her cubicle, she wondered, for the gazillionth time, how she had ended up writing for Aphrodezia. She had an MFA from the University of Iowa, the best writing program in the country. Only one percent of applicants who applied were accepted. She was one of the lucky ones, or so she thought, until she met scores of MFA grads slinging greasy diner food and working in florescent-lit convenience shops and university sportswear stores with U of Iowa on the butt of sweat pants. Despite evidence to the contrary, she thought she would do something more remarkable, more noteworthy with her degree. She would work as a freelancer and write for the *New*

Yorker, or maybe specialize in women's health and lifestyle issues and write for *Vogue*, *InStyle*, or even lower herself and write for *Cosmo*. Or she would get a fellowship to write the great American novel, which she already had an idea for—hacker brings U.S. to a standstill and single-handedly transforms society. No way would she get stuck selling horse, sheep, and cow-chow to Iowan farmers. No way.

Instead of hay for horses, she was selling romantica to housewives. Similar. Both types gobbled it up. The difference was that the hay gave life and the romantica led to brain death, especially her own. Some days, she felt she couldn't write one more foreplay scene if her life depended on it. Ironically, her life did depend on Rod's throbbing cock and Vanessa's wet pussy yearning for an engorged member. The days of pushing the limits on iambic pentameter and experimental prose were long gone. Now she just had to push out boners and orgasms.

When it came time to have real sexual experiences, she couldn't clear her mind of romantica clutter. Her mind could only produce clichéd scene after clichéd scene—sex on the beach, sex in cramped airplane lavatories, and sex in cabanas. She wondered if she would ever be able to rescue her sex life from the pages of romantica writing.

When most men talked dirty during love-making, she covered their mouths and said she preferred silence. What was dirty talk to them was shop talk to her. It transported her immediately to her dingy grey cubicle with no natural lighting, dying bamboo plants, and stale cups of coffee with floaters. There was one guy, though, whose dirty talk was so poetic and prolific, she would encourage his monologues and secretly record them. She wanted to have sex constantly, much to his delight, until he started to repeat his repertoire. Then she cut him off.

He left her countless voicemail messages: "Was it something I said? Was it something I didn't say? Did I say too much? Too little?"

As Alexis deleted his messages, she thought, *you said exactly what I needed you to say.* Then she used his material.

One time when Alexis was in her cubicle, writing the scene in which her protagonist, Chloe Cox, discovers that her man, Jack Hammer, was having an affair, she overheard Slater, her cubicle neighbor, breathing heavily. She hoped it wasn't what she thought it was. Perhaps he was merely experiencing sleep apnea, an asthma attack, or a sleep-induced breathing disorder. She stuck her iPhone earbuds into her ears and cranked Usher as loudly as she could, but then overheard a grunt and moan. Alexis IM'ed Jen.

Alexis: OMG. Did you hear that?

Jen: Hear what?

Alexis: Heavy breathing and a grunt?

Jen: I thought that was you. LOL.

Alexis: Very funny.

Jen: Must be a good scene. I dare you to IM him and ask to read it.

Alexis: OK.

Jen: JK. God, you wouldn't.

Alexis: I just did. Opening the doc now.

Jen: You HAVE to share it.

Alexis: Do I hear an offer for a four-course dinner at Zopitas? Margs and all?

Jen: C'mon. Give it up.

Alexis began to breathe loudly and moan softly.

Alexis: This IS good. Oh man. Who needs sex when you have Slater's scenes?

Jen: You're FOS.

Alexis: What's FOS?

Jen: Full of shit.

Alexis: Am I?

Then she sent Jen: "Like a spandex-clad superhero, he pulled off his sleep mask, grabbed her, and threw her down on the bed. He knew from experience that relationship talks never got her in the mood; they always led to her getting mad at him for some way in which he wasn't meeting her relationship standards. Kissing her was sometimes the only way to get her to quiet her thoughts. Her vocalizations began on the lower notes of the scale, pianissimo, a crescendo with each movement. The activity from the other room continued—thuds, bangs and groans, but it was now merely percussive background noise for Lilly's aria. Starting in the alto range, she moved to the second soprano range and then first soprano, and then back to alto, first, second, alto, first, second. The parts, now sung in staccato, were alternating faster and faster. When she hit the high C, she told him she wasn't finished. Good, he thought, neither am I."

Jen: I can't believe you asked him for his scene.

Alexis: I didn't. It's mine.

Jen: Very funny, you moron! And, BTW, that's not bad.

Alexis: Remember what they told us in Between the Sheets? It's OK to get aroused by your own sex scenes. In fact, it's a good thing because it means others will too.

Jen: Fine, but what do they say about arousal in cube farms?

Alexis: Trembling and stirrings should be shared with colleagues to inspire great writing.

Jen: Fuck you.

Jen and Alexis were attending the Romantica: Where Erotica Meets Romance 2018 conference at the Hyatt Hotel in Manhattan. After a full day of writing tips and tricks for romance and erotica writers, Alexis felt sexual-arousal fatigue and was looking forward to mood altering with Merlot. They plopped down at a table in the middle of the ballroom as the keynote speaker—an oversized middle-aged woman with a bowl cut and a too-tight canary-colored suit—discussed her 36th romance novel and her upcoming series about the adventures of a bisexual Midwestern housewife. Alexis kicked Jen under the table every time the canary laughed like a hyena on crack with her jelly roll at her midsection jiggling. *Not a good visual for romance writers,* thought Alexis. They had to quell their hysterics to the point of Alexis pinching her nose to make it stop. If they had broken out in uncontrollable laughter, they would have been the main attraction. It was likely the attendees were desperately seeking an upstaging incident. She would not be it. Not this time.

After the keynote, came the main course—bloody beef tenderloin with underdone new potatoes and overdone string beans. Peering at the sad trio, Alexis decided her main course would be the wine. As the writers, agents, and editors clinked, sliced, slurped and munched, Romantica's organizing committee congratulated each other for a job well done. Alexis likened this part to the Academy Awards when the award winners thanked everyone and their Aunt Gertrude for their successes. She always tuned it out.

Then Jen tapped her on the shoulder.

"What?"

"They're calling you to the podium."

"Huh?"

Jen whispered, "You're getting the Romantica Writer of the Year award!"

Alexis now understood the meaning of, "And then she peed in her pants."

"Shit," she whispered under her breath in the style of a ventriloquist. With all eyes on her, she scooted back her chair and donned a pleasant but professional expression, all the while feeling a little woozy and tipsy and wishing she were at home with her kitty cat—Tiktytac (an anagram of kitty cat) and a Katherine Hepburn flick.

Making her way up to the podium past a line of smiling suits with halitosis, she sidestepped next to the award-giver. Dottye grasped a cherry-wood plaque with a gold-embossed Romantica Writer of the Year, 2018: Alexis Townsend.

"Congratulations. You have been chosen by the Romantica Writers' Committee as the most extraordinary, outstanding emerging talent in the romantica genre. Would you like to say a few words of acceptance?"

Alexis stepped up to the podium and leaned into the microphone, trying to shrug off her tipsiness.

"Wow. This is highly unexpected. I had no idea…I'm not really prepared, nor do I think I'm the best by any stretch. Take Jen Ingalls or Slater Babcock or Maria Cortez, colleagues who are much more gifted. I dedicate this award to them for helping me blast through writer's blocks, push the limits of romance, and create my imaginative plots…" Then she was silent, like she had lost her place in a speech she hadn't prepared.

Audience members shuffled, cleared their throats, and took nervous sips of their beverages.

"God, what am I saying? I can't accept this award. I don't even believe in this genre with its formulaic approach and predictable endings, its moronic dialogue and dime-store sex scenes, its one-dimensional protagonists and antagonists. It's contributing to the dumbing-down of America and to its unimaginative renderings of sexuality. Oh, how fitting that we're writing for people who wouldn't know the difference between this and good literature. I'm sorry. Yes, they would. They like this stuff and would hate good literature, if they ever laid eyes on it, which they wouldn't.

"Who am I kidding? This is just a way to pay the bills. As a professor of mine at Iowa once said, 'A starving writer is not a writer at all. For how can you write if your stomach is growling and your brain needs fuel?' So, that's why I write romantica—so that I can put food in my stomach and a roof over my head. That is the one and only reason. I can't accept this award in good conscience. Please accept my regrets." She stepped down from the podium leaving the plaque with Dottye.

The audience was stunned into silence. The organizers, so perky and organized before, were dumbfounded. Then, someone in the back began to clap—solitary applause. Then another and another until at least a few dozen people were applauding. The applause was interrupted by tapping on the microphone. "Please, please. Show some respect." And the applauders promptly ceased.

Alexis escaped out the side door of the ballroom and bolted from the conference facility out into the streets of Manhattan. They were slick with rain and the lights were spotlights, featuring drizzle as the main act. Alexis ran down 42nd Street past Grand Central Station, over to Avenue of the Americas and into Central Park South before she realized she was running in stilettos. She couldn't feel her feet, her damp clothes, or even the tears streaming down her face. Perhaps it was because her tears were mixing with raindrops.

Alexis's office phone rang. She inspected the caller ID and didn't recognize the number. Alexis Townsend," she said to the mystery caller.

"Oakley Ellington. We've met before."

"We have?"

"In a sense. Let me refresh your memory." Then he started clapping into the phone.

"Let's see—Zen retreat, Topanga Canyon, 2016. What is the sound of one hand clapping?"

"Nope."

"I'm sorry. Your auditory clue is lost on me."

"Romantica 2018—Hyatt ballroom. You left in a rush."

"Oh, god. If you're calling to reprimand or shame me, I'll be suddenly unavailable."

"I admire your integrity."

"You do?"

"Very much."

"Not so much integrity as falling apart in the throes of hypocrisy." She suspected he was trying to butter her up before he roped her in. She had been approached by agents before, wanting her to go out on her own and do freelance romance. "Thank you, Mr. Ellington, but whatever you're proposing, I probably can't accept. Aphrodezia offers a regular paycheck."

"But you're miserable. You said so in front of hundreds of people."

"I'd be more miserable without a way to buy pizza and beer and the occasional indie flick."

"What if I told you that you could eat sushi and drink sake every night?" He stopped speaking, maybe waiting for her not-forthcoming answer. "Hear me out, then tell me what you think of my offer—OK?"

"OK." She was removing the nail gunk from under her nails and flicking it into the trash can.

"Would you consider leaving if I told you I could get you a book deal?"

"Listen, Mr. Ellington, I'm not in a position to go out on my own on a whim and a gamble."

"What would you say if I told you that Random House is offering you six figures—no strings attached—to write whatever novel you want?"

Her office chair slump straightened. Her heart and mind went haywire. "I don't get it. How is this possible? Don't people have to finish novels—especially first-time novelists—before they get offers? I mean, I'm a trashy romance writer. Why would they take such an uncalculated risk on me?" Alexis's mouth had hijacked her brain and she was talking a mile a minute, while her brain was stuck in a state of 911 with a spiritual conversion bent: *Oh my god! Oh my god! Oh my god!*

"I've been following your work for, oh, a couple years and you are a damned gifted writer. I can see beyond the clit lit—forgive me for being crude. I pitched you—just you—to Random House and they took the bait!"

"Is this some kind of prank? I mean, did someone put you up to this? Was it Jen? Slater? Is it April Fools' in October?"

"Nope, this is the real deal, Alexis."

"This is the part where I wake up and realize it's all a dream—right?"

"Nope. Here, listen to this."

He played a voicemail message for her: "Oakley, this is Soriah Delecor from Random House. We want to offer Alexis $200,000 for her first novel, the genre of her choice. Think you can get to her before someone else does?"

"So, what do you say?"

Alexis stared at her latest composition:

Monica unzipped Rusty's Wranglers with her teeth and slipped his jeans to the floor. Then she used her tongue to remove his tighty whiteys.

"You've got one damned talented mouth," he said as his pony came to life and trotted along his belly.

"You ain't seen nuthin' yet. I've just one request, Rusty."

"What's that, pretty lady?"

"Keep your cowboy hat on. I've always wanted to ride a cowboy."

Alexis asked Oakley to hold for a minute while she took time to consider his offer. She put the phone on mute and stared straight ahead, no longer seeing the dialogue from *Rusty's Red Wagon*. She catapulted out of her chair, leapt onto her desk, flung her arms up and screamed at the top of her lungs, "Yee-haw!" An exclamation that would have made Rusty proud, had he been a real character. Then she did a faux-Irish jig on her desk. She had no awareness that all her coworkers had awoken from their erotica-induced stupors. She didn't see that her boss was making her way over to her cubicle to tell her to chill out. She didn't detect the creepy guys from accounting sneaking a peek up her skirt. She didn't notice that Jen was gawking at her like she had finally cracked from writing one too many foreplay scenes. Neither did she see that Slater was giving her the thumbs up, even though he had no idea what she was yee-hawing about.

She bounded off her desk, picked up the phone, unmuted Oakley and said, "I accept!"

Alexis finally understood the meaning of "tears of joy." The joy, streaming down her cheeks, trickled into her lips. Saltiness had never tasted so sweet.

Static Breakdown

Misty did an abbreviated pole dance on the red and white striped pole in front of the shiny red booth. As she pulled away from the pole, she swung her head around, her waist-length blonde hair with dark roots aloft, and pursed her bright fuchsia lips.

"Stop being such an attention whore," Josie said as she spanked Misty's behind playing peek-a-boo with her black-pleather hot pants.

"Well, shouldn't I be what I am, bitch?" Misty slipped her leg straddling the pole down to the red and white checkered floor of the diner. Her D-cup store-bought breasts—everything revealed but her nipples—jiggled like Jell-O as she jumped down. She loved to tell people she had a drive-through boob job; they sliced her open, plopped the water balloons in, sewed her nips up, and voila! Kick-ass instant boner boobs.

The male customers froze mid-bite and fixated on the tit show. If one of their wives had choked on her blue-plate special right then and required the Heimlich maneuver and an ambulance, they would have never noticed.

"Whatever, Mistletoe. God, your parents must have been psychic or something, only smooching under plants is tame compared to what you do."

"More like psycho. And, please, don't ever call me Mistletoe. I abhor that name."

"Abhor—huh? Are we using congressional vocab now that you're doing big-time politicos?" asked Josie.

"Abhor was the word of the day, loser. Congressional—ha! Who talks? And when we do it's definitely not high and mighty. It's creep-o, geezer dirty talk."

Misty slid over on the shiny red diner booth—the plastic cold on her bare legs. "Brrrrrrr—it's fucking freezing in here."

"Well, if you'd ever wear clothes, you might actually be warm for a change."

Once seated, Misty took in the ambience of the diner—chrome tables, fixtures, and red-and-white striped everything. "This place looks like a fucking candy cane. I could just lick every last drop of it," she said as she pantomimed licking and displayed her tongue stud. "Maybe if congressional dudes had candy canes for cocks, I'd like my job better."

A red-and-white striped waitress walked up carrying two chocolate milkshakes with sprinkles and plunked them down on the table. She nodded her head toward a table of four guys and said, "They wanted to buy you girls drinks. I told them this wasn't that kind of joint. We don't have martinis or nothing like that and they said, 'What do you recommend, then?' I told them all girls like chocolate milkshakes. So, here you go."

As Misty and Josie glanced at the milkshake-buying dudes, one of them pumped his arms and stuck out his tongue.

"Oh, god, you know what that means; I told you to cut the exhibitionistic crap. He wants a piece of you, Misty."

Misty eyed the lizard up and down and said, "He can't afford me," and then laughed before sticking her index finger into the whipped cream, wrapping her juicy lips around it, and sucking. Then she leaned over and slurped her milkshake so quickly, she got a cold headache. "Brain freeze!"

Oh-oh-ohhhhhhh-oh-ohhhhhhhh-God-oh-God-oh-God! Orgiastic sounds emanated from Misty's purse.

"What the fuck, chica?" asked Josie with a palm-up hand gesture.

Misty mouthed "love line," holding one finger in the air to buy time with Josie. "Ooh, you do it to me so fine." Misty's forehead furrowed. "Whatever, dude. I'm not in the mood for you to go all parental on me. Hit me with your best shot. Client 15. Now? Three big ones? I'm there!" Misty was quiet for a minute. "What's that clicking sound? Are you clicking a pen or something? Don't you hear it? Oh well, ciao." Misty hung up.

"Have you ever considered that your phone might be bugged? They're onto you, girlfriend."

"Highly doubt it. Damn, the twisted sister asked me if I had changed my O-ring, yet. She said it attracts unwanted attention. Isn't that an oxymoron?"

"See you *are* getting all congressional on me. What the hell is an oxymoron? An idiot on oxycontin?"

"Sister, sister, it's a figure of speech that combines two normally contradictory terms," explained Misty.

Josie pursed her lips and pantomimed high and mighty.

"Gotta push off. Big-ass fish on the line." Misty slurped the rest of her milkshake until the sucking sounds were so loud even Josie gave her a look.

"Gotta suck every last drop of sweetness to prepare for the sour shit."

Josie made an icky-poo face and dug into her milkshake with a long spoon.

Misty pried herself from the red plastic booth, kissed Josie on the cheek and said, "The Love Gov is on his way— no doubt with a bad case of blue balls. He's always all backed up when he needs to see me spur of the moment like this. Oh, and as always—mum's the word on this stuff. Cool?" said Misty.

"You don't have to say that every time I see you." Then Josie stood up on the booth's shiny seat and play-acted disclosing Misty's secret to the diner customers.

Misty punched her and then flashed a smile and a Jersey gang symbol, flipping her hair as she walked through the field of gawking men.

"A-one-a-two-a-one-two-three-four." Misty kicked off her band's jam session in the garage of her parental unit (aka Mom) who was flying solo after the royal asshole, Cougar, (aka Dad) burned her mom with a blowtorch. On purpose.

When Misty recounts the story, she rolls her eyes, fiddles with her tongue stud, says "flying fuckwad," referring to her father, and then adds, "Like any of us buys that he mistook her for a machine part. And when we don't fall for that BS, he claims his face shield fogged up. Now if your face shield fogged up, would you just blowtorch with abandon, or would you turn the friggin' thing off? Fucking genius."

The drummer, keyboardist, bass and electric guitarists in Static Breakdown played five bars and Misty shouted, "Stop! Stop! Stop!" She moved her mic stand to the left of her mouth. "You cats have to give it more meow. That sounded like a fucking lame garage band."

"Isn't that pretty much what we are?" said the keyboardist, staring at her cleavage. Her breasts were bulging out of her top-of-the line leather jacket. She liked to wear it with nothing underneath. It made her feel like Cat Woman. Plus the feel of the leather against her tits was a huge turn-on.

"Hey, dudes, let's rename our band Lame Garage Band," said the drummer, who, for once, wasn't stoned.

"Logan, we are not going to waste our entire jam session on band renaming like we did last time," said Misty. We all went with Static Breakdown and that's final."

"*You* went with Static Breakdown," said the lead guitarist. "Everyone else wanted Toxic Jesus. We don't even know what Static Breakdown means."

"And, can you explain Toxic Jesus?"

The lead guitarist said into his mic, "*Toxic Jesus* is a societal commentary on the way we're being poisoned by religion in this country."

"How about you write an essay on the topic and send it to someone who cares? So, what's this going to be now, a Misty gang-bang session? Are we going to sing or just shoot the shit? Cuz if the latter, I'm going inside to record my solo single. I don't have time for you monkeys."

"OK, dudes, let's jam," said the bassist, who had a mad crush on Misty.

"Ask her about her trip to St. Tropez," teased the keyboardist, who was jealous of the bassist because he thought the plucker and Misty had a thing going.

"Ooh-la-la, St. Tropez, Misty!" said the lead guitarist, "Who took you there, your sugar daddio?"

"Back off, and no, I went alone. I don't have a sugar daddio. I paid my own way, you morons."

"This chick's got a serious stash of cash somewhere. But where, I wonder. Under the floorboards?" asked the drummer.

"It's like those people who win the lottery, but keep living the same miserable existence," added the keyboardist looking around at her mother's junked-out, burned-out, smelly garage.

Misty repeatedly hit her forehead with the microphone, making loud crashing sounds. "If this is going to be a Misty slam session, I'm outta here. What will it be?"

The guys in the band wanted to do her so badly, they had to vent their sexual tension somehow. Unlucky for her, they played hardball. Lucky for her, nothing got through her thick skin.

Her cell phone chimed Aerosmith's "Walk this Way," the stranger ring. She pulled it out of her pocket to spot check the number. It said, private. She answered, "Yo," and said nothing for the rest of the call. She went from ticked off to confused to shaken in a matter of minutes. She clicked her phone off and started crying. "Oh my God. I have no idea what just happened."

"What did they say?" asked the bassist.

"That guy just threatened me. He said if I don't leave the country—actually the continent would be well-advised—that I'd live—or maybe not even—to regret it." She looked up at the band members. "What should I do?"

"Sounds like a mafia call, if I've ever heard one. What do you have yourself mixed up with, Mist?" asked the keyboardist.

"Nothing. I've done nothing—that I know of. Maybe I sleepwalked and committed a crime or something. That happens to people."

"Maybe you should hire a private eye or even a bodyguard," suggested the bassist.

"Maybe," she said teary-eyed and sniffling.

"We'll be your bodyguards," said the lead guitarist, making eye contact with all the band members to build consensus.

"Right on," said the drummer.

She ran into the lead guitarist's arms and started sobbing again. He clearly glowed with pride that she had chosen his arms over all the other instrumentalists.

"We'll protect you, babe. We won't let anything bad happen to the lead singer of Static Breakdown."

"Dude, listen," Lola (aka Misty) said, panty-less with a black peek-a-boo, plunging tank top. Client 15 was flying parallel to the ground—ramrod red—and panting, like a wild beast. His eyes were popping out of his head. He seemed on the verge of exploding at the sight of her round, soft bum peeking out of her tight T. Her clients loved the wrapped-up-and-bursting-out-of-tight-T-shirts look.

He started to bend her over and go for the slam dunk into the back entry, but she resisted.

"You can have it however you like it—on the rocks, straight up, with a twist, but we've gotta wrap it up. You know the drill, Gov."

"Listen, just this once. It won't do any harm. I'm clean. I've been tested. I haven't been anywhere—only with my wife. I promise."

"Yeah, but where has your wife been?" She laughed, suspecting that thought had never crossed his mind. "I refuse to give you the AIDS 101 briefing, Gov. Didn't you go to

Harvard? Aren't smart guys supposed to know this stuff? You are so fucking smart and so fucking hard." She made sure he saw her looking down at him.

He stiffened more under her gaze and touched himself like he couldn't believe how hard he was.

"Hard and brilliant," she said as she wrapped her arms around his shoulders and slid her hands down his arms, moving her hips up against his dripping cock. She swept his penis with her pelvis and then wrapped one leg around him. "What will it be? Are you going to govern me tonight or will I govern you? My pussy's getting warm, wet, and willy just being around you."

"I've never massaged your insides without the wrapper. Can't we just? Just for a minute."

She took his breath away by dropping down on her knees and forcefully taking his cock into her mouth. Misty tickled it with her tongue then thrust it deep into her throat. He let out a deep, hoarse moan as she massaged and sucked. She could taste his pre-semen; she knew he was close. It never took long; around her, he was a wild beast.

He ripped his penis from her mouth and grabbed her, trapping her with his embrace. He sunk his fingers deep between her legs and then jammed his penis inside her. It entered her part way and she pushed him away as hard as she could, and he fell back onto the bed.

"Hey, hey, we can do the rape thing, but only wrapped up and sealed. Wrapper rape. Read my lips. I don't do dangerous shit. She unwrapped the condom and, forced it onto his withering boner and then sat on him.

"It's not going to work," he sighed.

She leaned over his face, her breasts dangling out of her low-cut shirt. "Rip off my shirt and then suck my tits as hard as you can. Now!"

He tore her shirt in a lackluster fashion, but the more her breasts were exposed, the more his penis grew inside her. He ripped and tore more enthusiastically now, exposing her bouncing breasts and erect pierced nipples. Grabbing one and then the other, he sucked so hard it hurt her, but she kept rotating and rocking and tilting her pelvis back and forth— rhythmically and then forcefully.

His moaning was beastly and wild, not at all the sound of a man. Then as his penis mushroomed inside her, he exploded with an extended painful-sounding groan.

"Wow, Gov. See, wasn't so bad after all. Was it?" She sat above him and jiggled her breasts, then leaned down for a squeeze. "Let me know when you want me to extract myself and I'll pop off."

He was looking toward the diminishing light sneaking through the crack in the curtain-drawn window.

"Lola, would you stay with me tonight?"

"Don't you have to go home to your wifey?"

"Naah, she thinks I'm at a three-day gubernatorial summit."

"Summit—huh? Good one. Listen, overnights are double or nothing and then the morning glory is extra."

He thought for a minute, "That's eight grand for a slumber party? Shit, I should be in your line of work."

She laughed, thinking he didn't have the looks or, for that matter, the cock.

"A slumber party sans slumber, I'm guessing. Eight big ones for a sleepless night is about right. Thing is, you'll have to do a money transfer. I can't deposit checks that big, and I don't want the cash sitting around for wayward relatives to discover."

As they considered financial dealings over his shriveled, bagged dick, the familiar repulsion overtook her. One day, her financial dealings would be about her music, not about the rise and fall of random dudes' dicks.

"You sure know how to make a guy feel special."

"Not in the biz of doing the girlfriend experience—all warm and fuzzy and shit. We've got good-girl types who do that. I can recommend some—Tessa, Angel, Violet. I just know how to make a guy feel hot as hell and ready to rip, roar, and rumble. Got it?"

He laughed and cupped her breasts, bouncing each, one at a time. "You sure have tits that make a man want to fall in lo…fuck the hell out of you."

"Ha, ha. There's no way to fuck *all* the hell out of me. So, what will it be?" she said, resting by his side on her forearm.

He fondled and eyed her labia and clit, splitting her lips to peer inside at the hot pink flesh. Slipping his finger up inside her, he felt her swollen wetness; he looked shocked that he was starting to throb and grow again so soon.

"A sleepover," he said.

The next morning after romping in the hay for what seemed like days, Misty asked if she could use his laptop. She was getting bored with the Gov and ready to get back to her music, but she couldn't complain about the money she was banking. With the major cashola she scored from whacking guys off, she was planning to build a recording studio and launch a record label.

It mystified her why guys would pay so much for random chicks to whack them off, but it sure kept her living large. Misty figured the dudes could save a bunch of money if they'd just let their wives do the honors. She claimed that the daddy of all disturbing things about the escort biz was that dudes wanted to do girls their daughters' ages. Misty mostly suppressed that thought, but sometimes it would seep into her brainwaves while she was giving her signature BJ and it triggered her gag reflex.

The Gov handed her his laptop. "I don't mind you using it, but don't do anything incriminating that my wife might discover. And no viruses from porn sites," said the Gov.

"Chill, dude. I'm just getting on Facebook." She powered up in bed, laptop on her lap, and went straight to her Facebook fan page. She had just recorded and uploaded some tunes that she wanted her friends to check out.

"Oh my God! What the fuck?" She exclaimed.

"What is it?"

"I don't get it…I've had around ten thousand likes in the last 24 hours. Normally I get only 50 a day. Rock on!"

"Certainly your services aren't advertised on Facebook. Are they?"

"No. The Grande Geisha would hang me by my clit for that. Geisha Girls is all word of mouth." Then she donned her best voice-over voice and said, "Geisha Girls, a social introduction service that promises private, risk-free dating," then added, "Dating, my ass. With beautiful, educated companions of fine family and career backgrounds to persons of immense financial and influential affluence. Like I'm from a fine family background—ha! A blow-torching machinist and his white trailer trash whore. You didn't hear that—OK? But the PR crap got one thing right—you, Gov, are a man of immense influence.

"You politicos spread the word about Geisha—like wildfire I might add. No offense, but is everyone unhappy and bored with their wives or what? Do they not produce the goods? Are they frigid? Don't answer—none of my business, really," Misty said.

"You're right—none of your business," he agreed, slipping on his boxers and business casual attire—khakis and a blue button-down.

"You outta here, dude? Going to your gubernatorial summit?" She chuckled to herself.

"Just going out for coffee. Want some?"

"Hellz ya. I want all the works—caramel macchiato, extra whipped cream, caramel drizzled on the top," she said imagining the luscious concoction.

"OK, I'll be right back. Don't go anywhere. I can't stand to be away from you for even a few minutes."

She rolled her eyes, thinking the Gov was getting a little too close for comfort. "Right, I'll just step out for a quickie BJ delivery service. Time is money." She clicked on her music link and her voice rocked out in heavy metal screaming accompanied by guitar screeching. "So whaddya think of Static Breakdown?"

"Not my thing," he said, grasping the doorknob.

"Right, you're probably into easy listening and smooth jazz to soothe your frazzled nerves. You power brokers are all the same. No offense," she said as he opened the door. She detected some activity in her peripheral vision, but ignored it. The heavy metal music piped through his computer speakers and she was doing naked head-banging to her own band.

He dashed back in and slammed the door, breathing heavily and looking astonished.

"Quickest coffee run in the history of humankind. But where's my java?" Misty asked, still absorbed in Facebook. She didn't notice that he was leaning against the shiny executive desk, staring down at the floor, trying to prevent a heart incident.

"Holy Mother of fucking God!"

"What?" she asked absentmindedly.

"Paparazzi."

"Cool. Is someone famous out there?"

"Yeah, me. Holy Mother of fucking God!"

"Why do you keep saying that? Trust me, it's so totally uncool." She clicked on another tune, "Mystical Misfit," and waved her hand in the air. "What if I blast my tunes? Do you think I'll be discovered?" She finally glanced up only to find him red-faced and panting. If she didn't know any better, she might have thought he was on the verge of a heart attack or breakdown.

"Lola, they know."

"Who knows what?"

"They know about us. Someone leaked this to the press."

"Bummer, dude. Guess the party's over." She stared at the deflated condom in the trashcan beside the bed. Then she flashed on the phone call. *Was it one of the Gov's people? Did he brag to anyone? Had the Gov knowingly put them at risk just to get his rocks off?*

"I don't think you get it. This is the kind of scandal that...Let's just say that heads could roll—yours *and* mine *and* your escort service could be shut down by the feds. And this means we could lose each other."

"Did *you* spill the beans? I mean, sometimes dudes like to brag about their sexual prowess and shit."

"You really think my judgment would be that bad?"

"Your judgment didn't prevent you from using my services—oh, gazillions of times," she said, proud of herself for outthinking a governor.

He paced, running his hands through the few hundred strands of hair that were clinging on for dear life in the face of the genetic coding. "Perfect, just what I need—my girl becoming holier-than-thou."

"Your girl?" The words sent a creep-factor shiver through her body. "So, what do we do now? How can we get out of here?" Misty eyed the room for an escape route. "I know." She shuffled to the window.

"From the twelfth floor?"

"Minor issue. One guy, not too long ago, survived when he jumped out of a 20-story window. We could chance it. If I broke something, like my face, then I could get the reconstructive surgery I've been wanting. Cheeks, nose, chin and stuff."

"Shit, we should run off together." The Governor sat on the edge of the bed, hugging his abdomen like he was in pain, and started sobbing. "I can't lose you, Lola; you're all I have...I finally fucking feel something."

She had seen all kinds of clients—the guys who wanted a dominatrix, the ones who wanted anal, the men who wanted to tie her up, the ones who couldn't get it up with anyone but her, the guys who asked her to spank, slap, whip, and choke them. But never before had she had a client who broke down like a child. BJs and other sexual offerings came easily to her, but she had no idea how to comfort a man the age of her father going to pieces.

She set down the laptop and patted his shoulder. "Dude, it'll be OK. You'll go home to your wife, and it will all work out."

He sobbed and reached to hold her. She leaned away, keeping him at arm's length, and continued pat-a-pat-patting, which only made him grabbier.

Just then, her O-ring moaned and she spot-checked the caller ID. Incoming call: Grande Geisha. "Yes, yes, I know. You pulled the website? Wow! So, this *is* serious. OK, I won't talk." She hung up and looked at him. "Um, you might want to call your wife before she hears about it on the tube."

He didn't pay attention to Misty's advice. His first call was to his lawyer.

After six hours of being holed up in the Waldorf-Astoria, the first guests in the history of the hotel to ever feel like prisoners, Misty said, "I'm getting très claustrophobic. I'm hightailing it out of here before I go loco and *really* make headlines."

The Gov tried everything—including bribes and brainwashing—to convince her to stay, but she wasn't susceptible to sweet talk or strong-arming of any kind.

"Ciao, Gov!" she said as she looked back at him barricading himself in the bathroom.

As she opened the hotel room door, camera flashes blinded her. The photogs were just inches away. The reporters stuck microphones in her face, nearly taking out her teeth. They spewed questions in rapid-fire succession. The only one she could make out was, "How do you feel about being involved in such a high-profile scandal?"

Misty said, "One man's noise is another's music." Then she puckered her lips and flashed her signature gang gesture.

She left the hotel, the press still trailing her. She picked up the pace but they matched her step-for-step.

"Lola, what is your real name?" called out a reporter.

"Lola, were you Governor Levine's favorite escort? How many times did he use your services?"

"How much did Client 15 pay for you?"

"Is it true you've been offered $3 million to pose for *Hustler*?"

"Are you going to write a book?"

"What are you going to do with your overnight fame?"

Misty stopped suddenly and faced the paparazzi head on; they nearly collided with her.

"Here's the deal, dudes. I have a band called Static Breakdown. Check it out on Facebook. We rock! Watch for my record label Riotous Girlz."

Then she sprinted down an alley away from the media frenzy.

Misty shook her head as she watched the Gov on TV giving his resignation speech with his dick between his legs. His wife with swollen eyes and a sourpuss mouth, stood by as he apologized for his wrong-doing and for letting the people down. For what specifically, he did not say.

"He's not the first power broker to have to suck it up and won't be the last," Misty said like an expert on the topic to the boys in the band. "He should have been more careful to cover his tracks; these politicos get careless and think they're above it all."

The tube flashed a photo of Misty at the beach in bikini-wear. Static Breakdown responded with a chorus of "Cool, awesome, rock on, and what a hottie!" They were taking a breather from their Thursday night jam session to watch the news. Misty had to come clean with the guys as the story was breaking on every channel.

The lead guitarist with the don't-call-it-a-mullet hairstyle said, "Yep, I knew something was up. Threatening phone calls, trips to St. Tropez, expensive leather jackets. You had to be a complete moron not to put two and two together."

The other guys agreed that they had known, too.

"That's a crock of shit," challenged Mr. Non-Mullet-Head. "You guys had your skullcaps pulled over your eyes. I was the only one on the case."

The other guys threw couch pillows at the cocky SOB.

Her phone rang. She announced that it said "Private."

"Here, let me answer it," said the lead guitarist with his outstretched hand. "My first duty as bodyguard."

"It's all yours," Misty said as she threw the cell phone to him.

"Yo, what up?" the guitarist answered. "Who's calling?" Then he mouthed, it's him!

She reached for the phone. "Hey, Gov?"

He was crying.

"What's wrong, dude? Are you OK? I mean, I know this is hard and all." She walked into the bathroom and closed the door for privacy from Static Breakdown.

The Governor told her through sobs that the worst part of all of this was that he was never going to see her again. He said he hadn't slept since the last time they met and that he realized he couldn't live without her. Then he told her he planned to leave his wife so they could run off together.

"That's crazy talk. Listen, you don't understand. I'm not sure how to say this, so I'll just say it straight up. I'm not into you. Frankly, you're creeping me out. OK? I mean you're a nice guy and all, but the guys I'm into are, well, not old." She unzipped her jeans and clumsily peeled them to her ankles. "You know? It was just a gig for mega cashola. Capiche? Sorry, bye, Gov."

As she turned off her cell phone and sent him into cell phone oblivion, she peed, put her head in her hands and thought, how tragic, falling for his fucking escort. She flushed the toilet and bounded out of the bathroom. The band guys stood clustered in the hallway by the door studying the ceiling and rocking to imaginary music.

"Were you fuckheads eavesdropping? Get off on a girl peeing or what? Sickos, all of you. Men are just plain fucking pitiful."

The band guys had big question marks emblazoned on their faces and were uncharacteristically quiet, waiting for the verdict.

"It will cost ya," she said, holding out her hand and pumping her fingers in a cough-up-the-dough gesture. Then she laughed, shimmied, and wiggled her booty. "Oh yeah, the boys in the band have to pay for the privilege. Everyone does."

They looked both annoyed by her cockiness and in awe of her instant fame.

"Shit, you look like a bunch of UFOs in headlights. Don't you go getting freaky on me, too. OK, here's the lowdown. The Gov just told me that he's leaving his wife cuz he can't live without me. Tragic—huh?"

They nodded.

"And in case your curious minds want to know, no, I'm not running off with a washed-up political geezer."

She switched off the television with pundits and talking heads analyzing the implications of the scandal on Levine and his family and repeatedly showing Levine's agony-of-defeat face.

"Yada yada yada. I'm sick of this shit. Who's ready to jam?" Misty caressed the arms of the lead guitarist and keyboardist simultaneously and then tugged at the belt of the bassist, pulling him toward the garage.

Fourth Step Tango

My freshman-year boyfriend was a theater major from Fort Worth, Texas who did a southern preacher revival bit. His daddy was a rich oil man and Beauregard thought he could buy his way into anything. Unfortunately, no amount of money could buy acting talent.

Beauregard wasn't good at any parts but the preacher, and deep down, he knew it. In his various college productions, his character dying of AIDS was cloying, his melancholic writer was whiny, his cowboy was giddy minus the up. When college newspaper critics would trash him, he would hiss and spit and lash out—defending his fresh interpretation of the role. He may have been fresh, but like a steaming cow pie.

When Beauregard did his preacher routine, he would get the sound of fire and brimstone in his voice and the look of Moses on the Mount in his eyes. His horse choppers protruded as his lips disappeared into two thin lines. Spittle collected at the corners of his mouth, and his arms flailed toward heaven and hell. I couldn't watch the spittle; it triggered my gag reflex, especially when it stretched from his top lip to the bottom and wiggled as he spoke. Instead, I focused on his chaotic golden locks that sprouted above his gaunt, pocked face. Sweat of fury would stain his armpits and fly off his face. The room grew pungent. I had to stop inhaling through my nose and focus on mouth breathing. My lines, if I had any, were nasally. Good thing I usually had bit parts.

On one such enchanted evening, our stage was Beauregard's stark, very dimly lit bedroom in his off-campus house. Beau started the scene by lighting a match, illuminating the candle in front of him and then hovering above the candle like a beheaded ghoul in a rinky-dink haunted house.

I wanted to give stage direction. *Are you going for the Holy Ghost look, 'cuz you look more like a candlelit vampire?* But given that Beau wasn't open to stage direction, I refrained. His head traveled up from the candle—beheaded levitation—so that his tighty whiteys were illuminated. His penis package was now the star of the show, if the star is judged by where the light is shining.

He proclaimed, "The lawd have mercy on us all. He is a mighty merciful master. With God's grace flowing all around us, will you accept Christ as your Savior? Je-hu-sus died for your sins. Will you come to him now? If you don't take Je-hu-sus as your Savior, what will you do with your sins?"

"I will. Lawd have mercy," I said, playing along while thinking about the paper I should have been writing on the virgin and the whore in nineteenth century literature and art. I wondered which one Jesus would have preferred in his bed. And should I include that in my paper?

I was getting hungry, but Beau couldn't be interrupted, ever. You see, when he was in character, you had to be carried away by his performance. Or else.

On these occasions, you had two choices—spell-bound audience member or participating non-threatening cast member. That night, I chose to be an extra. My stomach was roaring. I hadn't eaten since black coffee at breakfast, if you call that eating.

"Allow me to give you some insight into the truth that God can save your wretched soul. He can save you if you are here today and have never been saved. God answers our concern about our loved ones by telling us in no uncertain terms that God can save them. Let me show you why I say that," Beauregard declared as his spittle broke.

Shouldn't have looked. Appetite suppressant. "Show me, show me," I cried out.

Just as I finished delivering my lines, imagining a group of extras responding in unison, Beauregard's eyes rolled back—flashing his whites—and I knew he would begin speaking in tongues. Although convincing, this part was the hardest to endure because there was no Jesus-is-Lord nonsense to argue with in my head. Jibberish did nothing for the development of my atheistic platform.

After 20 more minutes of the evangelical hysteria, he simmered down. I waited until the preaching aftershocks to raid the fridge. The only items that weren't scary were a stiff pizza slice on a limp paper plate, a forgotten Fanta orange soda behind the science experiments, and organic peanut butter with pooling oil.

While staring into the fridge—the light illuminating my face like a UFO with spotlights landing in a dark prairie—a question popped into my mind: Why in God's name was I with this guy? (I always asked this question after the revival routine.) Beau had sprung for my college expenses when my dad bailed on my tuition. (He and his new wife were having a love child.) Plus, Beau had taken me to Vail (I did a face-plant getting off the chairlift), Breckenridge (my tongue got stuck on my ski pole), and Copper Mountain (I nearly collided with a Sno-Cat) and bought me a leather jacket for Martin Luther

King Day (don't ask). And Beau was a really good kisser. Of course, I didn't have much to compare him to. I had only kissed a few guys and pseudo-guys in high school—Jason Berman (too much saliva), Carter Caruthers (too much tongue), Jim Dickey (too much dental hardware), and Sarah Starr and Jenny Graves playing Chuck Frye and Andy Robinson through Saran wrap (too much plastic).

Beau kissed like a pro from what I could tell—the feeling of Goldilocks sinking into just the right bed.

Armed with a pizza slice and peanut butter, I returned to his room. Beauregard was engrossed in a subtitled French flick.

"What's this?" I asked, attempting to tear a bite from the rubbery pizza slice. I felt like a dog chewing an old tennis shoe.

"*Last Tango in Paris.* I thought we would watch it before our trip to Crested Butte."

"Why? You know I hate subtitles."

"You'll like this one. There's a cool scene with butter. Classic. Quiet! I have to study Brando." He waved me away with his hand.

"Why should I care about butter?"

"Just watch." Somewhere between the rubbery pizza slice and the butter scene, my stomach began to gurgle.

91

Molly and I straddled the permanent ironing board in the dorm hallway—she on one end, I on the other. I wore my sorority sweatpants with Greek letters on the butt. Delta Gamma. I bought them because I liked the way they swayed with every step—Delta up, Gamma down, Gamma up, Delta down. They were the mainstay of my freshman-year wardrobe, when I was broke and had to beg for books.

Molly wore a University of Colorado sweatshirt and tight Levis. She swung her feet with painted hot pink toes. The halls of the dorm were empty, except for tipsy stragglers heading for a night of bed spins.

"So what do you know about *Last Tango in Paris?*" I asked her, while French braiding my hair.

"It's a butt fucking movie. It's supposed to be a classic, but it's lame. I don't get why the French chick slept with Brando."

"No kidding. So, if Beau made me watch it, do you think he wants to do it in Crested Butte?"

"Uh, yeah," Molly cocked her head and gave me a duh look. I felt butterflies in my stomach, thinking about "it." But what was "it" exactly?

"What should I take?" I wanted to ask her about "it," but couldn't get up the nerve just yet.

"Sexy underwear, perfume, and stuff."

"What do you mean—stuff?"

"Stuff that makes you sexy and hot."

"I don't have any of that. Just my cotton bikinis."

"You can borrow mine."

"Yuck."

We laughed.

"So, I mean, how does it work?"

"How does what work?"

"You know—doing it."

"Oh my god, you don't know?"

"No, I don't. And don't cop an attitude."

"Well," she said, leaning forward on the board and whispering, "he basically says romantic things, kisses you, pulls it out, and sticks it in." She looked around to make sure no one was listening.

"His thing, you mean."

"Yes, his thing."

"Is it creepy?"

She paused. "No, it's kinda cool."

"Does it, like, hurt?" I squinted my eyes imagining the feeling of a colossal tampon.

"Nah." Then she twisted her mouth in a thinking shape and reconsidered. "Well, a little, at first. Then it's awesome."

"And then what?"

"Then he groans, squirts, and it's over."

"And that's it? It ends after the squirt?"

"Pretty much."

It didn't sound very awesome to me. Popping, poking, squirting, and grunting. "Did you like it?" I smiled, trying to be perky about the poking.

"Of course." She glanced down and picked at her pink nails. "Who doesn't?"

"And then what happens?"

"It shrivels and he falls asleep."

"It shrivels? Like a worm?" I couldn't imagine getting naked with a shrinking slug. I was starting to wonder if this "ski" trip wasn't a terrible idea. But it was already booked.

"Oh." The butterflies that were flitting about in my stomach croaked.

A week after the screening of *Last Tango in Paris*, Beau jetted me to Crested Butte, a Colorado ski resort town, on a private plane. He wore a cowboy hat. I wore a grimace. I kept thinking we'd crash in the snowy peaks and never be found and have to eat each other to stay alive. But, I wouldn't eat Beauregard and his shriveled worm if my life depended on it.

The minute we set foot in the hotel room of the Butte Inn, he started acting strangely—like a character was coming on.

Oh, god. I hoped for just fire and brimstone; I knew how that played out.

He messed up his hair while making his way to the windows offset by the dingy floral maroon and green curtains. Beauregard banged his head against the window, and twirled around until his back was against the wall. He then slid down to a squat.

He was playing grief or depression, but it was a serious case of overacting, not to mention a cliché execution. Sliding-down-a-wall depression was not a fresh approach. But I kept my thoughts to myself.

"Everything outside of this place is bullshit," Beau said with his head in his hands.

I figured I'd better take my chances and jolt him out of character before he was too far gone. "Beau."

No response.

I tried again. "Beau, please."

"I'm not Beauregard; I'm Paul."

Oh shit, too late.

He pointed and said, "Go get the butter, baby girl. Bring me da buddah!"

"We have butter?" *How the hell did we get butter?*

"Yes, it's a prop for this scene. Don't make me get out of character again." He stood up and unbuttoned his shirt and unzipped his pants with a flourish.

95

I wasn't ready for that; I hadn't had time to slip into the sexy lingerie I had bought instead of books for my humanities course. "I'm not ready, Paul."

"Get ready!"

I grabbed the red silky lingerie out of my overnight bag and slipped into the bathroom. I wanted to surprise him.

"Bring me da buddah. Don't make me say it again."

I hastily threw on my lingerie while contemplating butter. Where was the butter? The fridge? I emerged in my naughty fire-engine red lingerie and peeked into the little fridge. I stuck my bum out for effect as I bent over. The refrigerator was empty, except for a solitary stick of butter. One fucking stick of butter. Then it dawned on me—one stick of butter for fucking.

We were doing *Last Tango in Paris.*

I should have known. Wait…Stop…I don't want to do it with butter, I wanted to say, but I didn't for fear of jolting him out of character. But what other choice did I have? I walked over to the bed he was sitting on and hid under the covers.

"The buddah, baby girl."

"Beauregard…I mean Paul…It's just that…Well, you see, I don't think this is a good idea after all."

"That's not your line, Jeanne."

"Cut! I don't want to be Jeanne. Cut!"

"We're rolling, baby. We're rolling."

I pulled the covers over me and held them down at both sides.

"Give me the goddamned butter!"

I slid one hand out from under the covers and held it out, a reluctant offering to an angry God.

He grabbed it and came toward me, ripping off the covers.

"No, I'm not doing *Last Tango*," I cried.

Ignoring my words, he pointed at my crotch and said, "Can I open that? Maybe there are jewels in it." He sat on top of me, trapping me underneath. Then he asked, "You afraid?"

I felt as if I would suffocate. I tried to push him off, but he wouldn't budge.

He reached into his underwear and out popped a flaming red chicken neck—perpendicular to the ground. I nearly gagged at the sight of it. He came at me like a heat-seeking missile.

"Turn over, baby girl."

I didn't.

"Now!" he ordered.

I still didn't.

"Do you want to turn over or do you want me to do it for you?"

97

As I turned, an ulcerous burning sensation spread throughout my abdomen. I closed my eyes. This was nothing like I had imagined so many times before—the holding, kissing, and caressing, basking in each other's arms. The sparkling, magical moment when I officially became a woman.

I felt a jabbing, greasy sensation in my anus. He was attempting the wrong port of entry.

"Ouch! What are you doing?" I said, lifting my face from the pillow.

"I thought I'd give you something different, something very *Last Tango*."

"Something different when I've never done it the right way?"

"That's not your line. Your line is 'Because you make me do things I've never done.' Now get it right, or we'll have to take it from the top."

In a whisper I said, "Because you make me do things I've never done."

"The fucking audio can't pick up your part," he seethed.

I began to shake from fear and anger—anger about him taking something precious away from me that I didn't want to give.

"Oh, god, baby. That's more like it. Let me into the Holy Family. Take me to the pearly gates." He took some butter from the stick and greased the adjacent tracks.

Then he jammed it in, just as Molly had explained. It felt like something was ripping down there. I didn't want to say anything, but I thought he might be doing permanent damage.

"Stop! It hurts!"

"Paul's got the butter, baby." He applied more butter and then banged against me thirty-three times; by the tenth, I felt absolutely nothing. Counting restored my sense of control. I reasoned that the thrusting couldn't go on forever.

I was thankful that the jabbing monster burst after the thirty-third thrust. After he grunted and his body stiffened—like I imagined rigor mortis—he rolled off me. I got up and went into the bathroom, locking the door behind me. I stared at myself in the mirror—my face still grimacing from the pain. But I felt nothing, just that I wanted to wash it all off. As I wiped myself clean, a pungent odor emanated from the washcloth. It made me gag. I scrubbed and scrubbed until the jasmine-scented soap erased the foul stench. But the jasmine only added a tropical scent to the murder scene. The corpse was still present.

With the vacant, longing eyes of someone behind bars, I pulled on my night shirt. I smelled the fresh scent of home—

freshly laundered in anticipation of this trip—my first overnight trip with a man. I just wanted to be surrounded by the fresh warmth of my laundry—in my dorm, on my single bed.

Problem was, I couldn't get any sleep there.

My roommate was a cowgirl. A real cowgirl from Happy Valley, although she didn't seem all that happy. I imagined a place where the girls ate rib eyes, twirled guns, said, "Howdy, partner," and messed around with boys in barns, hay in hair, wearing cowboy boots. They grew their girls real tall in Happy Valley.

Problem was she slept with a cowboy every night in our dorm room—with cowboy boots dangling through the bed slats. I always wondered if those things were hammered on like horseshoes.

Which is why I had wanted a boyfriend with a house in the first place; I wanted to escape the OK Corral in my bedroom.

The fresh laundry scent was seized by the wafting smell of a cigarette. Beau puffed, naked, wearing a cowboy hat, with a turkey neck limply displayed on the floral lime and orange bedspread. It looked like Thanksgiving at Grandma Mimi's house the year I became a vegetarian. I nearly gagged again looking at the hairless poultry neck. I didn't let him see, though. I was all calm and collected.

"I'm going to sleep," I announced, heading for the other bed.

"C'mon baby." He patted the bed beside him. "Sleep with me." The last thing in the world I wanted to do was wake up to his cockle-doodle-doo.

"OK." I pretended to fall asleep right away, which was a complete act. The best part was that Beauregard could never discern acting from the real thing. Tears welled up in my eyes and cascaded down my cheeks. No matter what, I told myself, don't sob or shake; he can't know I'm still awake. He might go for Act II.

Beauregard went for Acts II and III the next night when I was determined to not let him in again. He made me feel like it was my duty and his right—now that he had entered the pearly gates once, I owed it to him. I was a limp rag doll, but he didn't seem to care.

I don't know if it was the fact that my own father pulled the plug on my college tuition as he and his second wife started a new family or the fact that cowboys had invaded my dorm room, or a burgeoning case of insomnia, but I never refused Beauregard again, until he faded to black and was out of my life. I'm not sure how it happened; the details of my freshman year after the Unfortunate Butter Incident (as I referred to it in later years) were fuzzy.

Ten years later, Beauregard tracked me down in San Francisco, where I was working as a paralegal in the Financial District. When I picked up the phone, he was the last person in the world I expected or wanted to hear from.

"Hi, it's Beauregard. Beauregard Sturdevant."

Not to be confused with all the other Beauregards in my life. "Oh…Sure…Beauregard." A sick feeling coursed through my body.

"You're probably wondering why I'm calling."

"Listen, I'm not in the market for pyramid schemes, blue-green algae, or Jesus."

"That's not it. I'll get right to the point. I know what I did to you, and it was wrong."

"Yeah, the Unfortunate Butter Incident," I blurted without thinking.

"The what?"

"Oh nothing. It's ancient history."

"I'm doing a 12-step program and I'm on the fourth step—making amends. You were at the top of my list."

"Really? There's a 12-step program for taking people's virginity?"

"Not exactly. But you make amends for everything you did to hurt others."

"That's nice. So, you make amends, and then you can move on with your life?"

"Exactly. Can you forgive me?"

"To tell you the truth, I had forgotten until this phone call." What good was making amends when it reopened old wounds? Did they have a step for making amends for amends? "It was so long ago. Really."

"Well, you know what I did wasn't right—right?"

"Beauregard, please."

"I was an asshole then."

"And you're clueless now." I hung up. I didn't want to let him off the hook that easily. One simple phone call in exchange for my virginity? Not only that. All the years it took to discover that sex was not some violent, unpalatable event that men used against women. Making amends reminded me of Catholic confessionals. People could do all kinds of evil things and be absolved with a nod, a blink of an eye, or a simple confirmation. Thus, my atheism.

Five years later, a friend from college called to tell me that she had news about Beauregard. I was in my kitchen preparing chicken fried rice for my husband.

"He became a preacher."

I froze, spatula in hand, above the sizzling wok and let out a sharp, ironic laugh—the kind that comes out of your nose in a burst. "You're fucking kidding me." I plunged the spatula into the steaming stir-fry of chicken, rice, broccoli, and almonds and stirred with a vengeance.

"Remember his preacher routine?" she asked.

"God, how could I forget? It was the only part he could ever do well."

She laughed. "Apparently. Now he's playing the part for real."

"Real, my ass. It's just that he finally found a captive audience. Those poor unsuspecting bastards." None of the Lord's shepherds lined up in pews knew what I knew—that he was doing his bit for the butter—buttering up the saints so they'd open the gates of heaven when it was his turn.

I hung up the phone, threw my head back, and released a wicked laugh. What Beauregard didn't know is that all the butter in the world wouldn't get him to the pearly gates. I had struck a deal with the devil.

He would be doing the fourth step tango for eternity.

Fly Me to the Moon

Kylie had heard the news about Blake second- or third-hand. She couldn't remember which. But it was enough to spring her into action. In a shopping frenzy, she went to BestMart to buy a four-inch folding knife, and a deadhead mallet with hundreds of steel shot inside the canister. She also bought rubber tubing, Hefty garbage bags, mace, and a BB gun.

When she piled her selections on the checkout counter, the redheaded clerk with a neon orange tie glanced at the merchandise, at Kylie, and back at the merchandise.

"Planning to kill someone, ma'am?" His lips pulled back from his overbite to reveal a pair of bunny choppers that would have done Bugs proud, and he chuckled to himself as he scanned the items. "Just joshin' ya."

"It's not what it looks like," she said to the clerk.

"Normally, I'm not one to try to make sense of purchases. The way I see it, it's none of my business. But in your case, I put two and two together, and jeeeez."

"I've got a raccoon problem."

"You know we've got 'coon traps in the pest control section. If you want, I can get someone to bring one up." He started to page a floor manager to go fetch a trap.

"I have a method that works better. But thank you."

He gave her the once-over, imagining her way.

Kylie was twirling her hair, cracking her gum, and jiggling her leg. She checked her watch. 1800 hours. She only had 12 hours to get to the Orlando airport. She wished she could use a rocket launcher instead, but flying was her second best option.

"So you shoot 'em, mace 'em, clobber 'em, strangle 'em, gut 'em and bag 'em?" He laughed and scanned. "Ever eat 'em? I've heard some people make killer 'coon stew."

It was just her luck to have gotten Curious George masquerading as Bugs Bunny as her cashier on the night of such a critical mission. She looked at his name badge which said: HELLO! I'M BUSTER!

"OK, Buster, what is this? An inquisition? Just ring me up and get me out of here." She still had to stop at Wigs Plus and Save it for a Rainy Day.

The clerk looked as if he had just swallowed a goldfish and it was stuck in his throat—his eyes wide, his mouth closed. He was obviously trying to hold his tongue. The total came to $123.72.

She handed him her credit card.

He scanned it and turned it over to see the signature. "ID please."

She handed him her Texas license.

"Wow! Kylie Cross. Aren't you that famous astronaut who was on the space shuttle? Not Challenger. No, that one exploded. What was it? Discovery? I remember seeing you on TV in that orange suit with the black ring around the collar. So totally cool! Oh, and you're going on a mission to Mars soon. Right? Awesome!"

Kylie ran her fingers through her frosted, unbrushed hair. Normally, she liked being recognized, but tonight she wasn't in the mood to charm space fans. "Yep, that's me."

"What is it like? I mean, do you really snatch candy bars floating in the air and eat them? Is it like one of them bouncy castles, only like, you bounce up and don't come down? Man, how do you, like, go to the bathroom and stuff?" He stared at her, BB gun frozen over the scanner. "How do you sleep? Do you have to strap yourself to your bed?"

His passionate line of questioning triggered a memory in her. "Oh shit. Can you hold on a sec? I forgot something."

She turned in the general direction of the aisles. She started to take off and said, "Um, where are the diapers?"

"Baby items—aisles 13 and 14," Buster said without missing a beat.

"No, I mean adult diapers."

The clerk, who had let the murder theory go and had accepted but not embraced the raccoon story, was no doubt busy formulating another theory.

"Where are they?"

"Oh, adult diapers. Aisle 17."

Kylie came storming back with Super Plus Absorbency Depends, bikini-style in tow. Catching her breath, she plopped the package on the counter, and Buster added it to the total.

"Now your total is $141.17. On the card?"

"You know what? No." She reached into her purse and pulled out a stack of hundred dollar bills. She handed him two. As he opened the register, he appeared to be calculating more than her change.

"So these raccoons. You keep them as pets and put adult diapers on them so they don't muss up the house? Must be some big ass 'coons you got there." He snickered as he carefully counted out the change.

She sighed and snatched it from him. As he reached for a plastic BestMart bag, she grabbed the merchandise, stuck whatever would fit into her purse, and carried the rest. She bolted out of the store faster than the speed of light.

After buying a black trench coat at Save It for a Rainy Day, she headed to Wigs Plus, hoping they were still open. It was approaching 1900 hours. When she pulled up, the store looked as if it had closed. She jumped out and slammed her car door. The entrance was locked. She peered in, hot breath on the glass, and pounded on the door. Nothing. She pounded some more. A light came on in the front. An elderly woman wearing a perky blonde wig—1950s style—appeared, ambulating as slow as a sea lion.

Oh, c'mon. C'mon!

"We're closed!" mouthed the wig lady through the glass, pointing at the sign.

"Oh, please! It's an emergency. I promise to buy something!" Her heart raced more than it had during take-offs from the Kennedy Space Center.

The wig lady looked down at her watch, up at Kylie, down at her watch, up at Kylie.

"I'll be quick!" she yelled.

The wig lady unlocked the door and Kylie burst in. She ran over to the red wigs.

"What's the occasion, miss? In all my years, I've never heard of a wig emergency before. In this business, we generally say there are two reasons people buy wigs—style

109

changes and hair loss replacement. Do you suddenly want a style change? Or are you anticipating extreme hair loss by tomorrow morning?" The wig lady chuckled but then stopped when she noticed that Kylie wasn't smiling. Big question marks popped up in the wig lady's eyes.

"Oh no, nothing like that. Well, you see my best friend just started chemo and she's afraid no wig will suit her. I promised her I would find one she'd be happy with. She was so hysterical about hair loss that I told her I would return with her new hair in hand tonight."

"Oh, I see. I'm sorry to hear about your friend." Then the wig lady looked as if she were going to reveal a secret, such as liking to be tickled on the bum with ostrich feathers. Instead she winked and whispered, "By chance, is this friend you?"

"Not me. Thank God," Kylie said as she tried on Felicity, a red piece with an up-do and flying tendrils. She pulled off Felicity, and replaced it with Brigitte, a red shag. She adjusted Brigitte and posed left, adjusted it and posed right. "This one's good. Now I need brunette. I mean, my friend also needs a brunette wig."

Kylie blasted off to the brunette section. The slow-mo wig lady didn't make it to the brunette section until after Elvira. Kylie also tried on Britney, Candy, Cameo, Cassandra, Dotty, and Fantasy. She got lost in Fantasy—a thick, long, wavy piece—twisting and twirling, trying it at every angle. *Blake would like this one.* She imagined rolling around with him in satin sheets with her thick, illustrious hair covering his chest. He would growl like a tiger before and purr like a kitty after.

The wig lady grinned while looking at Kylie posing in Fantasy. "You like that one, miss. Do you think your friend will?"

"Yes, but I think she wants something lower maintenance, like Dotty." Dotty was short, sleek, and boyish. "Or maybe, ooh, Leslie—sassy and smart!" Leslie was a short bob style featuring a close tapered nape. The sides were brushed forward around the face for a flattering, layered look.

"Well, it certainly becomes you," the wig lady said. "You know, if ever want to go with a different look, that is."

Kylie was already in a different galaxy, imagining Orlando.

"So you're taking Brigitte and Leslie," the wig lady said as she lumbered over to the register.

"Oh, what the hell, I mean heck, throw in Fantasy, too." Kylie gathered up Brigitte, Leslie, and Fantasy and placed them on the counter. Her hand was trembling as she pulled out some cash.

"You know we get lots of girls on chemo in here. So sad. Personally, I think it's all the environmental toxins. The girls, knowing they'll soon be bald and all, hate to wig shop. It's so nice of you to come in for your friend. What a generous, thoughtful person you are, miss. The world needs more people like you."

Kylie felt explosively impatient, but she couldn't be rude after a shower of compliments. She had to let herself implode for the moment. "How much do I owe you?"

"Listen, I'm only going to charge you for two, since you are doing such a kind deed."

"Oh, you don't have to do that." Kylie paid and glanced at her watch: 1920 hours. With Brigitte, Leslie, and Fantasy in a bag, she flew out the door.

Kylie jumped up into her SUV and locked the doors, breathing a sigh of relief. She mentally checked off her list of provisions—wig, trench coat, mace, BB gun, knife, mallet, garbage bags, rubber hose, gloves, and diapers. Mission accomplished. Now the only things between her and Blake were a mere 900 hundred miles and that bitch, Trinity. If she drove at 75 mph with no stops, it would take her 12 hours. Only 12 hours before she met her destiny. *What a beautiful-sounding word.* If she and Blake ever had a little girl, she would name her Destiny.

She drove to an unlit portion of the parking lot to change into her disguise—trench coat, wig, and diapers. She was a master at changing clothes in tight quarters. Having lived on a space shuttle for 13 days, Kylie had become a mid-air quick-change artist. With gravity, however, this changing business was a little more difficult.

As she hit the highway, its dotted lines threading infinite monotony, she pulled out a handheld tape recorder and began composing a letter to Blake, "Astro-man, you fly me to the moon. And I don't say that lightly, or rather I do. As Astro-girl, I know exactly how that feels—weightless, floating on air, exhilarating, breathtaking. You are my zero-gravity man, Blake. I want us to go on another mission together. A space mission would be nice. But since only I was selected for Mars, how about a mission of sharing the rest of our lives? We were made for each other and she is interfering. But I'm going to handle that. Soon we'll be free and clear. Over." Kylie set the tape recorder down by her side—sitting at the ready—in case she was inspired. *Fly me to the moon. He'll like that.*

As red tail lights floated in and out, close and away, she remembered Blake as he had been in training. Working shoulder to shoulder on the mission controls, she took in his musky, sensual smell and swiped his hands, arms, and legs any chance she could get. She drank in his essence. With this heightened sense of touch and smell when around Blake, it made it hard to concentrate on the simulated missions. But being the radar-focused person she was, she had extracted

113

herself from thoughts of seduction, and zeroed in on the tasks at hand—operating the shuttle command center. Every minute of their 14-hour days prior to deployment was scheduled. With thoughts of space, Kylie had no time for earthly pleasures.

But now that the shuttle mission was completed, she wanted to make up for lost time. Kylie had to act quickly. Trinity might get to him first; she must intercept her orbit before it was too late. Trinity had to be placed on another trajectory.

Kylie's thoughts drifted to the shuttle simulator after hours. She imagined herself following Blake, his broad shoulders, large frame, and dark chocolate hair, into the simulated shuttle, closing the hatch, and manning the controls. He would float over to her and unzip her suit. Naked underneath it, her breasts would float upward. After detaching the suit and hurling into the air, he'd unzip his suit. In mid-air, caress her from below, embrace her from above. They'd tumble—zero-gravity acrobats. Twirling, twisting, flying, flipping, and rolling. Zero-g love-making.

Then Trinity entered the picture again. What if Blake had done this with her? Ire welled up from her core—molten lava ready to erupt and destroy everything in its wake. She glanced at the clock—2120 hours. Kylie felt pressure in her bladder and let it empty into her Depends. *No stops required on this mission. Astronaut training prepared me well for life.*

At 0600 hours on the outskirts of Orlando, Kylie donned Leslie and her London Fog. Strange. She was more nervous now than she had been before the shuttle launch, even though images of the Shuttle Challenger disaster had been dancing in her head as they blasted off. She figured if they went, they would go in explosive glory—forever documented in the annals of history. Plus, that was a mission of the head. This was a mission of the heart. Much more risky and treacherous territory for Kylie.

Kylie waited at baggage claim for Trinity. She spotted the home-wrecker weaving her way through the chaotic mass of travelers to the baggage carousel. Kylie's gaze followed Trinity, who appeared to have noticed someone she knew in the distance. Kylie's eyes traced Trinity's gaze through a crowd of arrivers, greeters and, luggage luggers. She spotted his broad shoulders, tousled dark hair, and broad smile. Blake! Trinity and Blake walked straight into each other's arms. Their lips locked in an interminable kiss. Kylie's heart pumped liquid rage through her veins, giving her the adrenaline punch to do what she had to do. But how would she get to Trinity without him?

He brushed Trinity's curly golden locks from her eyes and kissed her cheek; he held his lips there as though he was tasting her. Trinity's eyes closed in ecstasy. Kylie's squinted in fury.

Kylie had to eclipse this woman, but how? Then Trinity turned and walked away from him—to the restroom perhaps. Kylie pulled her trench collar up and followed, her bag in tow. Trinity was heading toward the elevators.

Perfect!

Trinity pushed the elevator button and waited. Kylie inched in until she stood directly behind her. Trinity entered. Kylie rushed in at the last minute. After the doors closed, Kylie, whose back was to Trinity, leaned forward and pressed the emergency stop with her gloved hand.

"Excuse me. What are you doing?"

Kylie faced the doors when she spoke, "I've been ordered to stop this elevator for security purposes."

"What security purposes? Elevator terrorism?" Trinity laughed. "Shouldn't we evacuate?" When Kylie didn't respond, Trinity yelled, "Get this thing moving or I'll press the emergency bell."

Kylie continued speaking to the elevator doors. "Listen to me. Your life is in danger; the only way you can remedy the situation is by staying away from Blake."

"What? How do you know Blake? Who are you?" Trinity pulled out her cell phone.

"I wouldn't do that if I were you."

Trinity poked at the screen.

Kylie turned to face her full-on, knocked the phone out of her hand, and pulled her knife from her trench coat pocket. "Stay away from Blake. Or else."

Trinity threw a punch at Kylie's face, but Kylie raised her arm and blocked it. Then Kylie pulled out her mace. She sprayed Trinity's eyes; they flickered as the acrid spray permeated the air and she gasped. She bent over, coughing and gagging, rubbing her eyes.

"I'm in no hurry. I'm going to keep you in here as long as I need to."

"People will notice I'm gone. Come looking."

"Who would?" Kylie asked, bracing for her to utter the name of her lover.

"If you stop now, I won't press kidnapping charges."

"Not until you promise to stay away from my Astro-man."

Trinity's hands flew up to her face. "Oh my God! Is that you, Commander Cross?"

"Well, what do you know, Commander Star? We meet again."

"You don't want to do this. Believe me. Your career will be over. You won't pass the screening for Mars with assault on your record."

"Fuck Mars! I get Blake or you're dead. Choose."

Trinity grunted as she attempted to peel open her eyes—blue pupils in a sea of red.

"Oh my God. You've really lost it. What happened to you, Cross? So far up and then so far down."

Kylie stuck a BB gun to Trinity's nose.

"Let me go now and this never happened."

"Let him go now, and you'll live."

"Think this through. You're a top-flight commander. Dedicating yourself to becoming an elite astronaut took dreams, guts, and brilliance. Don't throw it away, Cross." Trinity's bloodshot eyes pleaded.

Brilliant attempt at manipulation, bitch. "Ancient history as far as I'm concerned."

"You're a role model to women and girls all over the world."

"Cut the Sally Ride crap."

"Is this what you want your legacy to be? Female astronaut loses her marbles after shuttle mission? Insanity eclipses amazing feats every time."

"Insanity? The issue is you. Get out of the way of destiny." The elevator began to move down. "What the fuck?" Kylie pressed the emergency stop button. She held her breath. *Stop. Stop. Stop.* They continued to descend. She repeatedly slammed her fist against the red button. "Fucking stop!"

The door opened onto Kylie pointing her BB gun at a team of police officers, security guards. And Blake.

"Drop the gun!"

She dropped the gun but clung to the bag of goodies, for a split second imagining she could ram through the line of law enforcement officials and make a run for it.

Trinity ran into Blake's arms. He cradled her like he would never let go.

Kylie felt like she had been pummeled in the stomach. "Really. It's not what it looks like. I only wanted to talk to her. Make her understand."

Kylie's words fell on deaf ears as the law enforcement officers looked from the BB gun to the black bag, back to her face.

"Your name?"

"Kylie Cross."

"Ms. Cross, drop the bag. You have the right to remain silent. Anything you say can and will be used against you in a court of law. You have the right to speak to an attorney and to have an attorney present during any questioning. If you cannot afford a lawyer, one will be provided for you at

119

government expense," said the rotund officer as a petite officer handcuffed her.

Blake, still hugging Trinity to his chest and stroking her hair, was shaking his head.

Kylie wanted to rip every last strand of hair from Trinity's head, piece by piece, until her scalp was a bloody orb.

Blake took aim. "Cross, what a serious error in judgment. You had all the facts at your disposal. Why the hell did you do this to yourself, to me, to us?" Blake looked as though he would spit on her if it weren't for the presence of the law.

"You promised me, Blake. Remember?" Kylie's body pulsed and heaved as though liquid pain was surging up from her feet, legs and torso to the tips of her lashes. With her hands locked in hardware, she couldn't wipe away the streaming tears.

Kylie hunched in her orange jumpsuit across from Willem, her lawyer, in the prison visiting booth. If she was the moon, Willem was the sun. Kylie was a lunar landscape—barren, uninhabitable, frigid. Willem was on fire—the life force, coming to shine life-giving radiation on her moon. He was bald with rectangular glasses, a circular face, and a half-moon smile.

"I have to be honest with you. I took this case because I'm fascinated by what you do." His gaze shifted to the ceiling. "I mean your career. But until today, I thought we were screwed. I don't want you to pin all your hopes on this, but it is pretty fucking amazing."

Kylie, in a prison funk—aware of her bedhead, droopy eyes, slumped posture—could barely respond. "Try me."

"We did some digging and found a former NASA psychiatrist involved in a study in which they compared astronauts before and after space missions. In two percent of the cases, they found moderate to severe psychiatric after-effects."

Kylie perked up.

"The psychiatrist has documentation that NASA apparently has nowhere on file."

"Space cases."

"Exactly. Head in the clouds. Apparently NASA knows a thing or two about real space cases, but has kept it under wraps. Something about the effect of zero gravity on the brain and its fluids. Both can be permanently altered by space travel. Chemistry. Leading to personality disorders, psychiatric breaks, suicide, that sort of thing."

"Lovely. I'm legit, then. Good for the case. Not so good for me."

"No, no. It is good for you."

"I'll just be locked up with loonies instead of murderers. People who live in a padded hell versus people who live in a hard cold cell. Not sure that's an improvement."

"Proven insanity plea will keep you out of prison. Plus, juries love ruling against Big Brother if they think the people involved are going for a cover-up."

"I suppose I just royally fucked myself for Mars."

Willem's eyes shifted down to the concrete slab that connected them. If he had words on the tip of his tongue, they were locked inside his mouth. In lieu of words, he nodded.

"What would you say if I told you Blake made an important promise to me? Something relevant to the case," Kylie said.

A prison guard gave a two-minute warning. Every minute of every day was regimented and segmented. Strangely, being an astronaut had prepared Kylie for prison life—living in close, confined quarters with others in extreme inhumane conditions with limited provisions and bad food. She felt right at home.

Willem leaned in closer. "What kind of promise?"

"I covered for him on the shuttle mission, and he promised in return he would be with me. We almost didn't make it back because Blake made a miscalculation. I caught his error before its fatal execution. He knew it, and he said he

122

owed me his life. I saved his fucking life and mine, not to mention NASA's reputation. Not to mention the other eight astronauts aboard. Can you imagine two Challenger-type disasters? What would that do for NASA's image? Americans don't like exploding dreams and heroes. Now *I'm* the liability?"

Willem considered this. "Unfortunately, that doesn't justify a felony."

A burly female prison guard stated in a baritone voice, "Visiting time is over."

Willem tapped the table and said, "No worries. I think we've got what we need."

Kylie scooted back her chair and headed toward the cells. A prison guard tapped her on the shoulder.

"Excuse me, Miss Cross." The tall, buxom guard with a buzz cut who drove them like cattle to lockdown was uncharacteristically sheepish. She lingered and let her charges go ahead. Then she pulled out of her satchel a photo of Kylie—a shot taken before the mission—in her orange astronaut uniform. She was positioned in front of an American flag, holding her helmet, projecting a pre-mission glow. "Can I have your autograph, please?" She handed Kylie a pen.

Balancing the photo on her knee, Kylie studied it. *Who is that woman? That astronaut?* Then she signed the way she always did: "If you can dream it, you can do it. Kylie Cross, Shuttle Discovery."

As she scrawled her signature, it dawned on her. She wasn't sure why she hadn't seen it earlier. Trinity wasn't to blame for the ultimate betrayal. No, she had been an unfortunate distraction. Kylie was clear on her next mission, once freed from the confines of prison: destroy Blake. That was her dream. And she had every intention of doing it.

He Brings Me Flowers

A knockety-knock, a tappety-tap on her front door and Anna knew it could only be one silly boy with art supplies in tow. Chase's vision was to paint her *en plein air*, amidst the *Acer rubrum*. Before agreeing to something she might regret, Anna had said, "Translation, please."

"Outside under a maple tree," he said.

So far. So good. Anna imagined her jet-black hair set against the blazing crimson leaves. She wanted to use "crimson" instead of plain old red to impress Chase with her color palette knowledge, but couldn't match his seamless weaving of "en plein air" and "Acer rubrum" into everyday dialogue. She would appear stupid while trying to sound smart.

When he had said, "Keep it simple with a kimono—slip it on, slip it off," Anna said, "OK...Wait. What?" Where in the heart of Cincy might she pull off such a daredevilish act?

It wasn't sinful, exactly (no babies would be made in the process), but it was most certainly illegal. As a vegan Catholic girl, she had a reputation to uphold. Anna knew veganism didn't usually equal virtuousness, so she didn't know why she had paired the two. Yes, she did. She knew exactly why. Flaunting her veganism made her feel like she was someone. Like someone more than Anna.

Minutes before Chase was due to arrive, Anna's pre-studio-session clothing crisis had ended. She had lingered over her up-do, which could, in a flash, become a tousled down-do. Selecting perfectly sassy, vintage-y, sexy but not slutty was paralyzing. As his muse, she was the mood-maker, mixing inspiration with seduction. After a dozen wardrobe changes, she buckled under the weight of muse-dom. Gripped by drama, she felt on the verge (OMG, benzos!). Anna peered down at the mound of rejected clothing and collapsed in hysterics onto the pile. She had overlooked that she'd be taking it all off. Sometimes she was like that: so caught up in the moment that she lost track of her destination.

Anna would serve cherries (sweet), champagne (bubbly), and herself (sweet and bubbly) as the main dish. She had unloaded whimpering Asher, her two-year-old munchkin, and his care instructions at his dad's before he had consumed too many adult beverages to remember he had a kid. Romper

Room wasn't going to interfere with her sweetheart's muse. Not tonight anyway.

Chase had first called Anna his muse the night they met. Or, technically, the morning after. They'd shared a bark bench (dog park humor) and ecstatic-verging-on-orgiastic conversation for 24 hours straight. About their stalled marriages. About their spouses criticizing their artistic paths. About their yearning to break with convention. Just talk. Nothing else, except for interlaced arms, fingers, and legs. Anna wasn't entirely divorced yet and had a strict no-sex policy. At least for the first 48 hours. She knew it sounded non-discriminating, but if others could sense the buzzing, popping chemistry, they'd know it was incredibly so. Chase said his divorce was in the works, but didn't appear to have any policies, sexual or otherwise.

Anna had compiled a comparison list on her third-week anniversary with Chase.

The Husband:

- Likes chai tea.
- Likes to ski (which we don't do anymore).
- Bought standup paddle boards (which we've never used).

Chase:

- Is a creative genius.
- Paints like a madman.
- Loves cool vintage clothes.

- Dabbles in photography.
- Despises suburbia.
- Explores funky neighborhoods.
- Would rather be in Manhattan.
- Lets me ride tandem on his skateboard.
- Tracks the phases of the moon.
- Is obsessed with fortune cookies.
- Sings himself to sleep.
- Composes corny love poems.
- Adores kissing.
- Brings me flowers.

The list length disparity alone made her want to recoup the $45,000 dropped on her wedding. Admittedly, she had reveled in being queen for a day in a taffeta ball gown with attention, presents, and promises. She soon discovered all were fleeting. When she said, "Such is life," she felt a prick of pride at her emerging wisdom.

Chase knocked on her front door again, this time rhythmically. Anna ducked beneath the door's window and performed a shadow dance with her hands. Her theme: classy striptease. It was a shame Chase couldn't peer below the window. Her torso swayed in sync with her choreographed fingers. Her lacy taupe and beige vintage dress was classy-slinky-sexy, snug around her breasts and bum, flowing and flirting with her ankles.

From the other side of the door, a tune: "Baby, I'm-a want you. Baby, I'm-a need you. You're the only one I care enough to hurt about. Maybe I'm-a crazy, but I just can't live without…"

Anna squirmed to contain her tingling insides. She might have even squealed. She yanked the doorknob, poised to fling open the door to their reunion (after a 22-hour dry spell), but it wouldn't budge. "Hold on." Her rented duplex was a fixer-upper sans fixer. She tugged, jiggled, then slammed her hip against the damned thing; it shuddered and finally unstuck. This was not how she had imagined this scene—greeting Chase with a rattled expression. So not like the movies, except maybe a slapstick-y rom-com.

Anna stood face-to-face with a bouquet of wildflowers with protruding legs. "Is anyone in there?"

Chase peered through, his spiked blonde hair blending with the late summer blooms, as if his head were the bouquet's centerpiece. His eyes like marbles—facsimiles of the earth—blue and green swirls, his eyebrows animated exclamation points. He had starter jowls, but she tried not to dwell there. Besides when he smiled they disappeared. He wrapped his non-flower-holding arm around Anna's waist and guided her into the candlelit duplex. The last time she received flowers was when her soon-to-be-ex-husband proposed to her, vowing to pay her $130,000 student loans if she married him. She did. He didn't. Now she was student loan shark bait.

"My belle Annabelle." Chase's tongue-tackle was exquisite, except for his sandpaper cheeks. He pressed against her, his body firm and light, his scent sweet, earthy, maybe a hint of cinnamon. His mouth and tongue partnered for a flashy tango. Her tongue felt amateurish, alternating between exuberant lizard and limp sardine.

When her husband kissed her during their first year of marriage, it was simply to prep for his jackhammer routine. Eventually he said, "I'm just not a kisser. OK?" He might've clued her in before they vowed everlasting love and jointly plunged a knife into a seven-layer poppy seed wedding cake.

No one had ever called her Annabelle before. Not only was she incognito on social media, where Chase posted public love sonnets and haikus for her; it made her feel like so much more than Anna. She was tired of searching and not finding, of her abandoned life choices, of her wandering without the lust. Of a child not being the answer to fulfillment. But Chase made her feel sparkly, like someone precious. Like Annabelle.

He planted kisses in her hair, on her eyes, her nose even. When he ran out of uncharted territory, she said, "Hey, what was that song? The lyrics are so....yummy." *Yummy? Oh, god.*

"Bread."

"Is that a band?"

"Yeah. A seventies band."

"Will you play them for me sometime on your player?"

"You mean record player?

"Yeah."

"We can listen to them on YouTube."

"Oh, they're on there?"

"Of course, silly. They're not from the dark ages."

She didn't want the mood to go all different-decades awkward, so she hopped up to fetch cherries and champagne. "Stay right there."

She poured Chase a jar of champagne (her crystal flutes were being held hostage by her ex) and fed him a cherry. His lips were wafer-thin, but somehow expanded when he kissed. "Don't swallow the pit. Spit it out in my hand," she said.

"Don't go all mommy on me."

"Oh, god. Sorry. Autopilot."

After they fed each other tart cherries while polishing off the champagne, Chase left to get his oil paints, brushes, canvas, and easel. Anna had forgotten to take her Zoloft, so she popped pills with a champagne chaser—probably not recommended by her shrink, but he would never know.

"I'd like you to get down on your hands and knees with your cute butt facing me. Oh, and did I say I wanted you to undress? Minor oversight."

"Of course I knew about the undressing part—that's why we're inside. But are you serious? A portrait de la derriere?" She didn't remember much from high school French, but derriere had stuck with her. Leave it to the French to have the best word for butt, booty, bottom. No English words—slang or otherwise—did it justice.

"What's wrong with my face?"

"Too conventional. Oh, sorry. That came out wrong. Your face is perfect. It's just that the facial portrait has been done to death while neglecting the most sublime part of the human body."

Artsy, visionary, pushing boundaries. Although still warming up to Chase's artistic vision for her portrait, Anna wiggled out of her dress and tossed it aside. She clutched her iPhone like a security blanket. "Just as long as no one can recognize me."

"No guarantees."

"Will you please leave off the dandelion tattoo?"

Chase stepped away from the easel and traced, with his index finger, Anna's tattoo, the stem on her right buttock, and the dandelion seeds blowing up the arch of her back. "Like the wind, my Annabelle."

His touch spread from the dandelion to her warming, spreading insides.

Her phone dinged. Her texts were usually from him, so she was curious.

"Who's interrupting us?" Chase asked. "Here, let me see."

"It's nothing." Nothing was her mother, who Anna had just taught how to text. Bad, very bad idea. The text read: "Did you know Brenda went to high school with Chase?"

Crap. Yes. Anna knew Chase had attended high school with her half-sister, twice her age, but she was trying to forget. She definitely didn't want this fact to be a newsflash. Ever. She texted: *No worries. He just brought me flowers!*

But the dandelion moment had vanished. Her mother, half-sister, the priest, and a bevy of nuns had joined the naked studio session.

"You OK?" Chase asked before heading back to his easel.

"Yeah. Awesome." Pushing her palms into the hardwood floor, Anna arched her back and thrust her bum toward Chase and his easel as if to say: I'm unfazed, bold, erotic. In truth, she wanted to hide. At least shame wouldn't be visible on her backside.

After five or ten glasses of champagne, three or maybe a half dozen benzos (the competition's brand), a succession of white-linen airborne meals, and Paige was back in Cincy from China—Shanghai, Beijing, and Taipei. At least her body was back, as wretched as it was, her mouth parched and bitter no matter how much she drank, her eyes like sandpaper, her gut empty but woozy. Her body clock was somewhere between the Asia-Pacific, Hawaii, and California. Even though her heart raced, she could sense the beating was labored.

She kicked off her heels, twirled her hair into a messy bun and plunged chopsticks in at right angles. Before she spritzed her face, she winced at her supremely hung-over look—smeared mascara, matted hair, ghostly complexion, and puffy face. Jet lag gave her a sneak-preview of her crone years. She was counting on a good night's sleep to shave off a few decades. But a good night's sleep wasn't in the cards.

Paige dropped her luggage and spotted it—the one thing that didn't belong in her bedroom—thong underwear dotted with chopsticks and fortune cookies. She had never worn wedgy-style undergarments, let alone the Kung Pao variety. Her heart beat in her throat and suffocation felt imminent; a panic attack would take her down. She'd be dead on arrival; just her body and the thong. Each time her husband did this to her, it was like the first time. Each time, she believed he would discover it was her he wanted.

She was doing it all. And still, it wasn't enough.

Her husband had urged her to wear thong panties, especially as a treat after the unsexy girth of her pregnancy body. Her morning sickness, which was more like all-day sickness, meant sex was out of the question. Chase had suffered loudly during the long dry spells. Paige was mostly stretched too thin to fret over enticing undies; she was juggling the Zoloft Empire and bearing and raising three children while her husband explored his artistic self.

Paige bent down to pluck the Kung Pao panties with her chopsticks, quaking with rage. Although an experienced chopstick wielder, it took four attempts before she held them aloft at arm's length and dropped them into the wastebasket. She wanted to torch the damn things, but she'd probably have ignited a house fire. When the firemen arrived and asked her the source of the fire, she'd say a flammable fortune cookie thong had burst into flames. Go figure. Instead, her heart was on fire and nothing could extinguish it, not even sleep.

Paige usually gave herself 24 hours after an international trip before saying anything. With her head in the clouds and her feet barely on the ground, the truth flew out of her mouth. She said things she regretted, not because they weren't true, but because saying them jolted the status quo, fragile as it was.

This time was different. She dialed his store.

"Trashy Treasures. Someone's trash is another's treasure." An up-talking girl answered, as though the tagline were a question.

Fury gripped Paige's gut. She and Chase had agreed there'd be no employees as long as she was financing his still-fledgling second-hand store. Four years of trying to turn a profit by selling vintage hipster clothing and cool, quirky housewares had nearly drained their kids' college fund. It wasn't Chase's concern, though; claiming to be bad with money had absolved him of financial worries. He had playfully coined Paige the "green machine" and her fate was sealed.

"Who am I speaking with?" said Paige.

The girl giggled.

So unprofessional. Paige quickly realized her store-clerk assumption was faulty.

"Welcome back from the Orient," Chase intervened. "Are the Orientals ready to get drugged and happy?"

"It's Asia. Nobody calls it the Orient anymore."

The "shop girl" sang a little ditty off-key. If Paige could, she'd reach through the phone and wring her little non-musical neck, but she was probably just a girl—like their daughter Kayley.

Chase's belly laugh mingled with the girl's. Paige had always loved his contagious giggle until she realized it could be laced with sarcasm and scorn.

"How's my Lolli-lolli-pop-pop?"

This term of endearment with its percussive popping set Paige on edge. But she played along for fear of being a "buzzkill," prompting Chase to pursue extramarital liaisons.

"Is your vintage couch still for sale?" Paige asked.

"You're in luck. Someone took it for a test drive today, but didn't buy it. I'll cut you a friends' and family deal," said Chase.

"That's your bed until you ditch Miss Kung Pao Panties." Paige hung up before she could change her mind or say something she regretted.

Immediately her phone rang. She let it go to voicemail. It would be him, charming his way back into her bed. Only it wasn't. It was Zoloft calling. They always knew the minute she set foot on American soil. The VP of Global Markets asked if she had opened up the entire Asian market in one fell-swoop.

On impulse Paige returned the call. The minute the VP answered, she regretted it. She was on speakerphone addressing a room full of people—standing room only—who couldn't wait for her China report.

The VP said, "Zoloft is going to revolutionize Asia, and you're spearheading the revolution, the same way you spearheaded Europe. Watch out, world, Paige McNally is exporting happiness!"

"Let's not overstate the case. I'm no revolutionary. Trying to shift Chinese thinking around mental illness as a treatable condition is like trying to move the Great Wall. The thinking is that it's a curse—evil brought on by the afflicted. Hell, you'd think they were goddamned Catholics or something. I figure we'll need to do the pitch a dozen times before they consider making the switch from herbs to modern medicine," said Paige.

"But when they do, we're talking massive profits," said the VP.

"Even then, only a small percentage of patients will be open to Western medicine," Paige said.

"I don't get it. They're the most ancient healers. I mean, acupuncture originated in China. We have something to learn from them about treating mental conditions," said a meeting attendee.

"If needles were going to cure mental illness, they would've done it by now," Paige said. "It's exhausting trying to shift ancient thinking around brain disorders. Listen, I'm zonked. Can we pick it back up tomorrow?"

The attendees responded with a chorus of, "Sure. Of course. Get some rest."

Paige unpacked Chinese dragon kites for each of their three kids, staying with her sister while she was away. She nestled into her side of the bed. The covers on his side were tucked in, hospital style, the sage and lavender decorative pillows undisturbed. She messed up his side and settled in the middle so the bed wouldn't seem so gaping. When sleep didn't come, she hummed a lullaby—his nighttime serenade to lull them both to sleep. She rocked herself as her heart grasped for what might never be.

Chase's call never came.

Anna was sprucing up Chase's store displays, a chore that had turned into treating herself to his vintage finds. When the phone rang, Chase answered, "Trashy Treasures" in a lilting tone. It was the landlord claiming his rent was past due and, if he didn't pay, he'd tack on a hefty late fee. Chase told him it was on auto-pay, so surely there had been a banking error. He promised to look into it promptly.

The phone rang again, and Chase told Annabelle, "You answer it. Maybe you'll have better luck."

When Anna answered, the caller said, "You'd best be careful."

Anna mouthed, *It's her.* She was transfixed by her image in a grey vintage hat and a men's oversized shirt with leggings. She twirled around and the shirt flared out. She kicked her leg up for extra sassiness.

"You're not the first, and, trust me, you won't be the last," said Chase's wife.

Anna mouthed, *She's so bitter!* She suspected that bitterness hardened a woman and froze her features in irreversible bitchiness. She vowed never to be *that* woman. "Oh, really?" While tilting the fedora on her head, she did a quick bitch check in the mirror. *None detected. Thank God.* Her husband almost turned her into *that* woman.

Chase intervened when he suspected his wife was bad-mouthing him.

"Hi Paige."

"Have you found a place to live?"

"No. Why?"

"You've got a month."

"Is that a threat?"

"Just keeping you informed."

"C'mon. I'm your hubby. Am I some Zoloft headcase?"

"Leave off 'Zoloft' and 'hubby' and I think you've got it."

"So does this have anything to do with the rent payment on this store? It hasn't been paid."

"I closed that account. You'll need to open up your own." She hung up without any fanfare, no goodbye even.

"Holy shit." Chase dropped down on his couch (aka bed) and ran his fingers through his moussed hair.

"You OK?" asked Anna.

"Yeah." The last thing in the world he wanted Annabelle to know was that he wasn't making it. His store was on the verge of operating in the black, any day now. Launching a new small business was rough. It wasn't as easy as being a fucking drug dealer like Paige.

"She's hard on you. Isn't she?"

Chase nodded, interlaced his fingers behind his head, and closed his eyes.

Anna plunked down next to him. "Zoloft headcase, huh? I'm on Zoloft."

"You don't need that stuff. Your head is too pretty."

"I didn't need it until I said 'I do.' Such short words for such a long sentence," she said.

"You don't need to tell me."

"Why is she so upset if you've agreed to get divorced?"

"Because she doesn't want to."

Anna perked up and caught her reflection in the mirror while kissing him on the cheek. "What a lucky girl I am."

"And because she knows I was never really in love with her."

"Why'd you stay?"

"The kids mostly."

"That's a long time to be unhappy."

"And a long time to be deprived of this." He slid his hands from Anna's hips up under the large men's shirt to caress her breasts. She squirmed with delight. He disappeared under her shirt and helped himself to her nipples, taking each one in his mouth. He reappeared from under the shirt tent, sprinted to the front door to bolt it, and ran back breathless. "This has been my fantasy ever since you walked into my store." Anna blushed as he led her toward the fitting rooms.

"We can't fit in there. Well, I guess standing up we can." She giggled.

"I created my life and, oops, forgot to be happy," Paige said as Griffin, Director of Emerging Markets, her closest confidante, colleague, and sometimes barista whipped up a caffe mocha. "I'm good at everything except for happy, which is really the point. Isn't it? Perhaps some people are good at success and others are good at happy." Paige leafed through a thick report to be discussed in her meeting on emerging markets in Eastern Europe and the Baltics. She would have to wing it. She prided herself in being a skilled BS artist, a requirement when being a pharma industry exec. But when the rubber hit the road, there was no room for BS; people characterized her as exceedingly competent and claimed without fail she made sound decisions. Navigating legal and regulatory environments was her specialty. Under her watch, Zoloft sales had grown five-fold. It was true what everyone said; she was a stockholder's sweetheart.

"Maybe it's too damned late for me," said Paige.

"You're still here. Aren't you?" said Griffin, now working on the foam. No one had his touch of layering the foam and dark chocolate.

"Yeah. So?"

"It's not too late."

"But clearly I suck at happy, and incidentally at love, too. What if I discover that I've built an impenetrable fortress of suffering, moat, dragons, and all?"

"I'd catapult my way in."

Paige snickered, imagining Griffin soaring over the ramparts and splashing into the moat, bruised, soggy, determined.

"See the whole thing as a new venture."

Paige flinched. "Venture" was what her father called his attempts at entrepreneurship. She flashed on her father's final days, alone in a San Diego hotel room, a lethal mix of uppers and downers, after a chain of failed ventures and relationships. Since childhood she had been determined to never fail at anything. Now the F-word stared her in the face. A 25-year marriage that she was trying everything to save including a stint with S&M that landed her in the ER. The ER doc recognized her and winked while treating her.

"This is my blind spot. Spot is an understatement; it's a blind blotch," she said.

Griffin served her the caffe mocha paired with a chocolate-covered biscotti.

Paige dunked and crunched the biscotti. "I sure hit the jackpot, a guy still recovering from high school," said Paige. Chase had been her first love, a sought-after guard on the basketball team, a quick, nimble prankster. The cheerleading squad had a team crush on him, but he had snubbed perky pigtails and peek-a-boo panties for Paige. She swore off silly girlfriends, slumber parties, seances, and fart contests to go steady with Chase McNally. She was instantly the belle of her school.

"And, you, my dear, are still recovering, too."

"Really?" She scrunched her face, not wanting it to be true and embarrassed she was so transparent.

"You know what they say: lucky in business, unlucky in love."

"Is that so? Then they'd probably say: take the pills you're pushing. Headline: Zoloft couldn't save the Zoloft Czar."

"Ever think sometimes people take antidepressants not because they're depressed but because they're just unbearably lonely?" said Griffin.

She swigged her coffee. "Loneliness is really fucking profitable. And it's an expanding market. Maybe we'll put you in charge of that."

Later that fall, in preparation for his tête-à-tête with Paige, Chase jazzed up Trashy Treasures, color-coded the apparel, created homey settings with housewares, and uninstalled his art. He would reinstall his paintings the minute Paige left. He was going for the wow factor, eliminating anything that would prompt her to say, "It's not a store; it's an altar to your ego."

Annabelle, a self-proclaimed fashionista, who had an eye for window displays, had worked until his were eye-catching, show-stopping. The theme of the featured display was 1950s newsprint and media—the colors black, white, and red. If it bleeds, it leads. The female mannequins wore princess-line dresses made of newspaper with lacy red petticoats, fitted with red patent leather belts and stilettos to match. They flanked a table with a typewriter. Chase wanted to feature a typewriter—hip amongst budding writers. The male mannequin sported a fedora and was outfitted in a broad-shouldered and double-breasted suit. He was positioned next to a retro TV set in oak with legs.

The store bells chimed. Chase was caught off guard by Paige's early arrival. He was still arranging the shoe display by decade, which he thought was a clever merchandising move. *Learn about history while you shop for shoes*, he imagined saying to customers.

"Good to see some work actually gets done around here," said Paige dressed in a charcoal business suit.

"Paige-y!" Chase flung his arms open, a pair of shiny penny loafers (the easy breezy 1960s) in one hand. "These loafers are your size. Want to take them for a test drive? Come, slip these on, and I'll bring you some iced coffee— shot in the dark—just how you like it." He sprinted to the front door, flipped the sign over—*Back in 10*—and bolted the door. Customers could wait.

"I'd probably have to provide my own pennies—right?" said Paige.

"No. Pennies are on the house."

"Such a deal." Paige did a 360, taking in the new look of Trashy Treasures. "Looks like you've spruced this place up."

"Yeah. I think it's going to be a good quarter, a great year, actually."

"Where's your artwork?"

146

"Oh, I've decided to focus more on the store, ramping up sales, that kind of thing."

Paige glanced at her watch. "I've got 15 minutes. Let's cut to the chase."

"You know I love it when you say that, my Lolli-pop-pop-pop! You've no more time for your hubby than that?"

"Chase, stop, please."

"What?"

"The lollipop thing is annoying."

"Why didn't you ever tell me before now?"

Paige started to speak but waved her words away.

Chase served her coffee and slipped off her shoes. When he kneaded her feet, she didn't resist. Instead, her eyes fluttered to a close; her lips parted. He loved it when he caught a glimpse of the old Paige—the one who wouldn't reach for an umbrella in the rain but would frolic in puddles, taste snowflakes, and launch herself into piles of amber, tangerine, and crimson leaves. But any more she emerged only in flickers of light, shadow dances. If you blinked, she vanished; replaced by Power Paige with thick burgundy lipstick that persuaded, negotiated, intimidated, but never invited a kiss.

After the foot massage, he slipped on the loafers. "A perfect fit. See, I know you like the back of my hand."

"I suppose this is a fair exchange for my investment."

She laughed, but he didn't. It was a jab, one of the million points of pain that cleaved them apart. Each time she belittled his store—his opus—a piece of him died. If only she knew.

"Speaking of which, I wanted you to be the first to know about my new business model. If we finance this for another year, I can guarantee a profit. I've adopted a customer-based feedback model that drives my product acquisitions. Customers tell me what they want; I deliver it. I've changed my focus to strategic product placement."

"Right." Paige's eyes froze on a ceiling stain. "Do I need to remind you that last year you were $150,000 in the red, and the year before $100,000? You think you can make up that loss by selling typewriters, TVs, vintage costumes, and kitschy accessories for Halloween?"

"My assumptions are rock solid. I'll show you my spreadsheet." He made a beeline for his laptop on the checkout counter.

Paige watched him go. "No, Chase. We gave it four years—two years too many."

Chase mouthed words that he couldn't vocalize and paced in front of Paige and the shoe display. His charm offensive hadn't worked, neither had his brass-tacks approach. He straightened the shoes even though they were perfectly arranged. "You know this is my dream, and the only thing I know how to do. Other than art."

"Guess it's time to retool. You've received all the customer feedback you need. Maybe the vintage thing is over." She slipped off the penny loafers and stepped into her pumps.

"Shit, Paige. You've never understood my dreams, even if you threw money at them. You've never really seen me, because of the Paige show. Paige earns this award and that bonus and a promotion, and Business Woman of the Year, and White House honoree. There was no room for me. I've lived in the shadows of the almighty Paige."

Paige stood up, slinging her purse over her shoulder. "And I'm supposed to feel guilty because you failed? You did that all by yourself." She elbowed past him as she rushed out of Trashy Treasures. Chase wanted to call her all kinds of names that would provoke a reaction and force her to recant, but she seemed different, detached. His head was filled with obscenities, but his heart wouldn't oblige. It remembered who they once were.

Chase didn't flip the entrance sign over: *Come on in for a Trashy Treasure hunt!* Even though a few customers knocked, he wasn't in a customer-service mood. He had poured so much of himself into his store, and the community had failed him. Potential customers were too enamored with cookie-cutter stores like Pottery Barn and the Gap, factory consumption for people with no imagination. His revenue numbers didn't reflect the love and artistry that had gone into creating his upscale secondhand store. One person understood his vision, though, and that was Annabelle. She adored the store as much as he did.

Chase rehung his artwork, perfectly aligning each piece. Surrounded by his mixed-media works, *Fortune Cookie in Pieces*, *Impaled Ballerina*, *Clown Head Explosion*, *Turtle Devours Dove*, he felt worlds better. His painting of Annabelle was yet unnamed; it would come to him in a flash of inspiration. Although he had never actually sold a painting in his store, he felt his work provided an edgy, contemporary backdrop to his vintage offerings—a rich fusion of old and new.

Chase placed the needle of his only working record player on vinyl. The speakers crackled and played "Feels Like the First Time" by Foreigner, circa 1977, the tune that played when Chase and Paige had lost their innocence to each other, a song that Annabelle wouldn't even recognize.

He missed her—the Paige he once knew—the vulnerable girl with pigtails and patched overhauls who tried to appear tomboy tough. The girl who would duct-tape her father's hands together when he was blacked out so when he awoke he wouldn't hurl vodka bottles at her mother.

This Paige didn't need him or anyone. Chase felt unseen in her invincibility.

Anna wanted to surprise Chase at the shop. He had seemed a little glum. She guessed he needed a little Annabelle infusion. After they had spruced up his store displays, all motivation had drained out of him. When she asked him what was on his mind, he said he was rethinking things. She hoped "things" didn't include her.

Anna and Chase swapped marital sagas, her husband and his 101 ways to belittle her; for an uncreative guy, he excelled at being an inventive verbal abuser. Chase withstood his wife's disdain for his life as an artist. They held each other on their respective artistic paths, he as a multimedia artist and she as an evolving creative spirit.

That day, she wanted to sneak up from behind, cover his eyes, and say, "Guess who?" Of course, it would be obvious it was her, but who cared? How could she slip in without the store bell chiming? She'd go in the back service door. She loved the service entrance because it was a holding area for all his new merchandise. She got first pick of the treasures. She slowly unlatched the door and crept in amongst the sewing machine, a table with red vinyl chairs, a mini jukebox (oh, she wanted this!), an old-fashioned rotary pay phone, and other odds and ends. She found a black sequin hat and gloves that she slipped on.

Anna hid behind the door to the shop. She overheard Chase's voice and a girl's giggle. She peeked. He was helping the girl try on hats. Not only was he not glum; he was animated.

"Let's put money in the jukebox," said the girl.

"Sure, sweets," said Chase.

Sweets? Who's this girl? Anna's racing heart made her dizzy. She steadied herself against the aquamarine fridge.

"What's 'Twist and Shout?'"

"The Beatles," said Chase.

"That's a goofy name."

"Oh, give me a break. You know the Beatles."

"Ghostly geezers who should hang it up. Why don't aging rockers know when to call it quits? Don't they know they're creepy?"

"Trust me. They're still cool. Here, let me show how to do the twist."

They started writhing in front of the jukebox in silly hats; he in a fedora and she in a newsboy. In two-toned shoes, he gyrated, looking all last century. The girl doubled over in hysterics. That prompted him to act goofier by twisting on one foot and then the other, wagging each leg in the air.

"You know you twist little girl," he shouted. "You twist so fine."

Was she his other girl? Anna's heart seized up. Chase and the girl were so in sync. *I shouldn't be here.*

"Wait. I've got something for us." To Anna's horror, he ran straight toward her, for the service entrance, too quickly for her to hide.

"Anna...belle." He was out of breath.

"I should go."

"No, come on in. We're just screwing around." He grabbed Anna's gloved hand and pulled her into the store. The twisting and shouting morphed into standing and staring. She sure as hell wasn't going to twist and shout with some chick angling for Chase. She held her elbows next to her chest and braced for the worst.

"Annabelle, this is my little girl, Kayley."

Holy crap. His daughter? Kayley looked grown up, blonde, and gorgeous. "Hi. I'm Anna...belle. Oh, I guess he already said that." She hid behind her hand.

"How do you know my dad?" asked Kayley, avoiding eye contact.

Anna pled with wide eyes for Chase to intervene; he hadn't briefed her on standard operating procedures for interacting with his family. He hadn't shared much about his kids, only that he had them, but nothing more.

153

"Oh, Annabelle helps me around the shop. She did the displays. Aren't they incredible?"

Anna was pleased that her handiwork was being recognized. She didn't feel proud about much, but she knew she had an eye for beauty.

"Cool. But I thought mom said no employees," said Kayley.

"She's not. She's a volunteer. Isn't that sweet?" said Chase.

Kayley glanced at her dad, then at Anna, and at her dad again. She scrunched her face in realization that Anna wasn't a do-gooder shopgirl. Then her face-squeeze morphed into a jaw-drop. "Oh, my god. Seriously, Dad? You and Mom aren't even getting divorced. She looks like she's my age. Eww."

Anna had never been eww'ed in her life. She had always done the eww'ing. She was frozen in her sequin hat and gloves on the checkered floor with the flashing jukebox, not knowing how to respond to eww from the daughter of the man she adored, whose marital status was in flux. She wanted to fling the hat and gloves at his goddamned feet and flee.

Anna shot a glance at Chase. He shrugged. That was the best he could do? Was Kayley right about his marriage? She sure as hell hoped not. Then she caught herself—wasn't it wrong to root for divorce with this girl's future at stake?

"It's not what you think." Chase grabbed his daughter's arm as she blasted toward the door.

"Don't touch me!" Kayley jerked free of his grasp. She whipped her newsboy hat Frisbee-style onto the floor and ran out the door, slamming it behind her. Chase followed her and they stood outside, her arms crossed, his arms flying. Anna knew her twinge of jealousy was inappropriate, but it didn't diminish the feeling that Kayley's place in his heart was undying and hers fleeting. That she perceived his daughter as competition was wrong. She knew it, but couldn't stop the feeling.

Paige was heads down, tweaking her strategic plan for China when she was summoned for an emergency meeting. *Sorry, emergency isn't written into my calendar.* She snatched her laptop, thinking she could tinker with the plan while her colleagues yammered on about the "crisis."

The meeting attendees clutching digital devices positioned themselves around a table fit for a king's feast.

"I'll not mince words. We've just learned that CJ's wife committed suicide," said the chief operating officer. The room gasped. And then a chorus of oh my god, how awful.

"Yes. It's a nightmare. Aside from the personal tragedy, the company has a massive PR problem on its hands. The

155

CEO's wife was on Zoloft. And, as you know, she was a spokesperson for our product."

"Who knows about this?" asked an attendee.

"Somehow it was leaked to the local press," said the chief operating officer.

Paige's phone chimed. It was a text from Kayley: *I need to talk, like now!*

She ducked out of the meeting waving her phone as evidence. "Family emergency." She dialed. "What is it, Kay?" Her heart raced; her mind clouded with imagery of disaster scenarios befalling her family: injury, illness, assault, kidnapping, or worse.

Kayley sobbed and couldn't get her words out. "It's Dad."

"What happened? Is he OK?"

"He's fine, but I'm not."

"What's going on?"

"Are you getting divorced?"

"No, sweetie."

"This girl walked into his store—a girl about my age. I think they're dating or something. So creepy."

Paige inhaled sharply and paused. She paced outside the conference room.

"Mom?"

"I'm still here. Listen, I know it's upsetting, but no matter what happens, I'll be just fine." Paige nibbled her only remaining fingernail. The rest were nubs.

"OK," Kayley sniffled.

"This is what men do when they need to feel young again."

"What about my feelings?"

"This isn't about you. Dad's having a mid-life crisis." Paige wanted to say, *and taking us along for the ride,* but she bit her tongue.

"If I tell him to stop seeing her, do you think he will?"

"I don't know. Your father is young at heart, but he has some growing up to do." *That's the understatement of the year.*

"I hate him."

"I know, but he's doing the best he can. It doesn't mean he doesn't love you. When I get home, we'll make chicken tostadas and watch a movie on Netflix—your pick. Sound good?"

When Paige rejoined the meeting, she learned that the suicide cover-up was now her baby. Her take-away: never duck out of a meeting; you will always be assigned the most unpleasant tasks.

Back in her office, she asked Griffin to help her since she was in the throes of family drama. "Why the fuck is this my responsibility?"

"Because you're the Zoloft Czar." They stared at the blinking cursor on her blank computer screen.

"So how about this? CJ had bipolar disorder all along and antidepressants, when given to bipolar people, can worsen their symptoms, even leading to suicidal impulses. Zoloft wasn't the right medication for her," Paige said.

"Perfect. A diagnostic error. Pin it on the doc," Griffin said with ta-da-we-found-the-answer hands, even though it was Paige who had.

She noticed that his fingers were elegant, his hands intelligent, confident, sensitive. How she could glean all that information from hands, she wasn't sure. If one could tell fortunes with lifelines, couldn't one also infer personality traits from fingers?

"At least we shift the burden away from us." She fluffed up her hair. She could tell by the flat, lifeless feel of her head that it had turned into a bad hair day. Any day that goes on long enough will. "But this approach could backfire if his wife's health information, although protected by HIPAA, is revealed. The doc would be motivated to throw it back on us."

"Oh shit!" His gaze shifted from the computer screen to Paige.

She could see concern in his searching eyes, and she didn't like it. It meant she was vulnerable, hurting. It meant she was doing a bad job of hiding it.

"You OK?" he asked.

"Yes, of course." She nodded and placed her hands on the keyboard to get back to the task at hand. *Focus. Type. Stop. The. Pain.*

"You don't always have to be strong," said Griffin.

Don't. Please don't. She was being yanked under, the pressure behind her eyes piercing, her stomach in a vice-grip, a cloak of descending doom. She couldn't save Zoloft. She couldn't save her father. She couldn't save her marriage. She couldn't save herself.

Paige spun her chair away from him. Her body was no longer hers. A wave rose from her legs to her stomach, queasy, dizzy. She convulsed, sputtered, trembled. Time and space collapsed as she heaved the darkness within. A tender warmth on her shoulder. She shuddered at his touch.

"It's OK," he said.

"Go. Please go."

"You need someone. Let me stay with you." He handed her tissues.

His presence took the edge off, like salving the hurt with warm honey, a sweet succulence. An unfurling of the knot of tiny little hurts, an opening in her chest. She was suspended

159

among clouds, floating in deep blue, no safe landing spot, but she trusted her weightlessness.

Paige rested her head on the back of the chair and pinched her eyes closed. "God, I'm exhausted."

"I know."

Could she hear his heart beating, or was it hers? Was his breath tickling her neck?

She spoke to the ceiling. "You should see Chase's internet footprint. He has posted slews of tragic photos of himself—his silhouette cast on buildings, his half-naked body in the rain, his face obscured by his hand, and broken fortune cookies with sarcastic captions to girls with hidden identities. His life-long project has been the erection of Chase McNally," said Paige. The minute it came out, she regretted her word choice.

But Griffin didn't go there; he matched her tenor. "No wonder. When you're with someone in love with himself, you'll lose every time."

Paige spun around to squeeze his knees; it took him seconds to see what she had endured for 25 years. "No shit."

Griffin brushed a strand of hair out of her face and leaned in for a kiss. She responded, halting at first, surrendering to the succulence of his lips, a gasp. She covered her mouth, both as a defense and in response to the electrifying sensation spreading from her lips to her belly and swirling between her thighs. No one but Chase had ever made her tremble. Perhaps because he had been her one and only.

Paige stopped by Chase's store to drop off Kayley's soccer stuff. She shivered as she approached the store, not because of the chill in the air but because of having to face him. She swallowed the dread in her throat and vowed no softening.

She plunked the bag on the front counter. "Feels like the First Time" was playing on the record player. *Oh, god. Not that song.*

Chase was glued to his laptop. "I'm starting to sell my paintings. It was a clever merchandising move to show them here."

"Listen, Chase…"

"I had this epiphany. I mean, if I really go for life as an artist, I can make something happen—right? I realize I've been a shmuck, an asshole, you name it, fill in the blank. You've held our lives together and, thanks to you, our kids are great. You've been waiting for me to get my shit together and I think it is finally happening. I'm becoming the artist I've always wanted to be." He threw his hands up— abracadabra, magician's hands.

"Chase…"

He put his index finger on her lips.

Paige recoiled.

Chase tried to snatch her hands.

She busied hers with the vintage salt and pepper shakers displayed on the counter so they wouldn't be tempted to wring his artistic neck.

He produced a bouquet of roses and lilies, clearly proud of himself for thinking of flowers. The aroma assaulted her, a cloying toxic scent; the petals like cactus thorns. If accepted, another bouquet of broken promises.

Paige shook her head with her eyes closed.

He set the flowers down in front of her. "Just in case you change your mind. Listen, can we go steady, like old times? Only this time…this time as a grown-up man." His slumpy posture straightened. Man posture.

Paige fiddled with the salt and pepper shakers, Mr. Peanut with a top hat and cane. She felt a slight tug; these were the words she had been waiting for. He pivoted and so could she. This time would be different. He would finally swear off his dalliances. She stifled a sardonic laugh.

"What's funny?" Chase asked with a furrowed brow and pursed lips, a half-pout.

"You are." She inspected Mr. Peanut, never looking up. She could clearly see that the set was a piece of trash, so far from a treasure. It wouldn't sell for much, if it ever sold. Her

162

blood pressure almost spiked until she realized she could let it go. "I'm sorry."

"Is there someone else?" Chase's voice tapered off.

There was so much Paige wanted to say, could say. She had run out of words, out of breath to alight the words. "It's just not you anymore." She tapped Chase's hand as though he were contagious.

He shimmied around the counter and pulled her in for an embrace.

She could've pushed him away, the guy who had stolen her heart, the father of her children, the boy who could never be a man. No matter how hard she tried. She had none of the same longing; he felt wooden, like one of his mannequins. She pried him off and then lifted the needle off the record, scratching it. She might have done it on purpose. Her hands shook, not from grief and loss, but from the surge of energy that comes from being freed of a force that has long held you down.

Paige couldn't look at him. If he was crying, she didn't want to soften. If he wasn't, she didn't want to feel the sting. "How much for the shakers?" She wanted a keepsake. A pair of nuts was perfect.

"On the house."

"You'll receive papers to sign. Might want to hire an attorney." As Paige left, she glanced back. He was posing for a selfie with a painting of a woman's butt. She cringed. Her husband's *Selfie Avec Derriere* would soon be posted for the world to see.

She had left Mr. Peanut. *No going back now.*

Paige had been so immersed in Chase's world; she hadn't noticed snow pirouetting down from a puffy frosted sky. Snowflakes like tiny frozen stars sizzled on her flushed cheeks. She thrust her tongue toward the sky so she could taste winter.

Chase had left her a voicemail message, "Hot-as-hell Annabelle, would you stop by the store? I have a little something for you."

Little Asher would be with her, so it had to be G-rated but, yes, she would. Anna didn't tell Chase that she had a little something for him too.

He surprised her with a bouquet of roses and lilies. Did he not know that lilies were the flower of death? She whiffed and sniffed until she was light-headed; it would have been love, passion, and generosity all rolled into one if he had really meant it. Asher ran to the play area and zoomed and varoomed a double-decker bus while Chase and Anna leaned against the checkout counter. Her boy was much more adept at truck, car, and train noises than talking.

Anna admired a set of salt and pepper shakers shaped like peanuts with top hats and canes. "These are cool. They made stuff so much better back in the day. Can I have them?"

"Sure. All yours!"

"My belle Annabelle, I wanted to see if you'd go steady with me."

She rolled her eyes. "How's that different from what we've been doing?"

"It just makes it official." He posed with outstretched maître d' hands. He was tone-deaf to her mood.

"If it means you'll hide your Bumble profile."

"I've been meaning to..."

"While you're at it, Tinder too."

"Sure. Sure. It was a just-in-case kinda thing." He stepped out from behind the counter.

"Just in case what? You met someone better?"

"Jeez. Nothing like that."

"Want to play Truth or Dare?"

"Heck yeah," Chase said, clearly thinking the mood was shifting away from chastisement. "Dare."

"Actually, we're starting with truth. Did you hit on my sister Brenda while you and I were seeing each other?" asked Anna.

"No way. But, who knows? Maybe I was buzzed and don't remember. Whatever, it means nothing at all."

Anna paused, waiting for something more, an expression of regret, a reason to stay, but if Chase's conscience was plaguing him, it didn't show. "That is seriously 'eww' like Kayley said. Is it Brenda you really want or someone else I don't even know about?"

"It's you."

"I can't be absolutely sure and trying to figure it out is a serious buzzkill." He put his arm around her and patted her butt. She swiped his hand away.

Asher dashed over clutching the bus. "Mama OK?"

"Mama's fine but we're going. Put the bus back, Ash."

"Annabelle, we can talk through this. I need you more than you know."

"I thought I needed you, too, until I realized the best thing that ever happened to me wasn't. My heart is like the fucking unfortunate fortune cookie in your painting." She was, once again, a single mom in dive digs, waiting for divorce papers. No frills. No thrills.

"Speaking of which, I'm taking a painting with me."

"You are?"

"Yes, my portrait." Anna signaled air-quotes.

Chase shook his head. She could see he was bracing against tears. Perhaps he did feel something for her, or more

166

likely it was self-pity. She couldn't get pulled back in. It felt good to discover what she was capable of. She had never before walked away from something she thought she wanted.

Chase meticulously covered the canvas with a plastic trash bag. Anna wanted to say, don't bother. She left the lily-rose bouquet on the counter, stuffed Mr. Peanut into her pocket, and air-kissed Chase's cheek as he handed her the painting. She took Asher's hand and exited to the sound of tinkling bells. Anna maneuvered her Honda hatchback behind an adjacent shopping center and parked in an alley by a dumpster. In one fluid movement, she grabbed the painting, emerged into the frosty air, and flung it into the dumpster with extra gusto. Her gaze followed the arc of the piece through the snowflakes and listened as it clunked into the canister—echoing finality. Then she reached into her pocket and hurled Mr. Peanut. The shaker shattered as it made contact with the dumpster.

As Anna drove home, she wept softly so she wouldn't alarm Asher. He was such a tender-hearted boy; whenever she was visibly upset, he would crinkle his face and cry, "Mama boo-boo? Mama boo-boo?" The day her husband moved out, Anna told Asher that Mama had a heart boo-boo. He wanted to see it, so he tugged at her shirt. She planned to explain that heart boo-boos were invisible, but figured that was too advanced for a toddler. She showed him her heart

167

and he said, "Boobie, not boo-boo!" They toppled over in giggles.

They had each other. Maybe that was enough.

Chase trailed Annabelle, not stalking but investigating. As he watched her chuck his painting, the sting of her discarding his piece was almost equal to that of the end of their affair. It was her loss that she couldn't recognize a masterpiece. He performed a flying leap into the empty dumpster and retrieved his work. It was his favorite; no way would he let it end up in a city dump, although it would be a cool photo to post on Instagram. *Derriere in detritus.*

He noticed the remnants of Mr. Peanut, picked up the pieces, stared at them, and stuffed them into his pocket.

Back at the store, Chase rehung the painting over the checkout counter and stood, arms crossed, peering up at the Post-Expressionist-style derriere set in bold primary colors. He'd need to install some track lighting to showcase his work. One of his customers wouldn't be able to resist the lure of this piece. His price tag: $3000 or maybe $4000. He'd shoot high and work his way down.

Chase settled onto his couch/bed, cozying up with an army blanket—scratchy but sturdy. "Trashy" wasn't a bad crash pad after all; he'd just have to hide from customers that his store was doubling as his home. As soon as he turned a profit, he'd go house hunting for a place with space for an art studio, maybe even a carriage house with exposed brick walls.

Before bed he fired up his laptop and jumped on his social media account to see how many likes he had netted for the butt painting selfie. 86 likes and 30 snarky comments. Score! "Nice ass. Can I meet her?" "Asshole selfie?" "A pair of asses?" "Redundant, dude." "Want to do mine next?"

Yes, as a matter of fact, I do.

Crafting his online persona had become his favorite pastime. Chase was precisely the person he had always wanted to be—artsy, hip, sardonic, with a touch of childlike innocence. He posted another selfie with his butt painting. This time he went for: melancholy, mysterious, pissed off, and slightly aloof with a noir photographic effect. Chase shot several takes before striking the perfect pose. The caption: *I loved her butt she left me.* That would be the title of his painting. A little long, but he had always pushed the boundaries of art.

He'd surely awaken to an outpouring of likes.

The Magician

I didn't know much about him, only that he was a magician with salt, pepper, and purple hair that spiked as high as his pointy beard extended down low. In his profile picture, he poses with a patch-eyed parrot on his shoulder and a wand in his hand. I hoped neither would make its appearance at dinner and that he'd downplay the magician thing. In his note he said he liked my impish name, Fiona, and my far-off look; he could see mischief in the glint of my eyes, wanderlust in my nose, and trepidation in my mouth—a study in contrasts. He had said it made him want to explore the disquiet. I loved that he used the word "disquiet." I studied my photo and saw little of what he claimed to see. But he was right about one thing: my long-held fear of being swept off the ground at the mercy of the wind was written on my lips.

I suggested a place where we wouldn't run into anyone familiar—a Korean restaurant on the outskirts of town frequented by Asians, who might just see us as two quirky Caucasians rather than a pair of desperate internet daters. I'd have bi bim bap—beef with egg, veggies and rice—and, if it didn't go well, I'd wash it out down with super spicy kimchee.

For me, a corporate content curator (aka: a creative writer who wanted to eat), the magician was internet date number 99, not that anyone was counting. I wanted him to be 100; I felt there was something enchanted about a magician being my 100th, but the 99s kept canceling or were no-shows. I finally accepted that the magician was meant to be 99; if things worked out with him, I'd never move into higher math. The triple digits past 100 made me feel despondent— like from there the numbers would expand into infinity—a blur of badly balding; charming but acerbic when drunk; tall, dark and creepy; loveable but destitute; wealthy but stalking; sexy but penny-pinching; affable but kinky. My sky-high numbers would be an aching testament to my inability to couple, to pair up, to be anything but alone.

My friends told me the best approach was to scrap internet dating (losers, players, and flakes) and angle for widowers. But how? Was I to frequent mortuaries or graveyards searching for the handsomely bereaved? And what if the grieving guys had actually loved their deceased wives?

I'd be competing with a ghost. During lovemaking, I'd wonder if she was hovering above us poised to use her ghostly powers to haunt every ecstatic moan, especially during climaxes. I simply wasn't game for phantasmal voyeurism.

I strolled into Dae Gee Pig Out! Dae Gee means pig in Korean, but most non-Korean-speakers didn't know the translation, so weren't bothered by: Pig Pig Out! I scanned the place for the magician but only saw a sea of Asian faces. The pleasantly plump Korean hostess wearing a jade green pantsuit handed me a laminated menu with pictures and said, "Just one?"

"No, actually there will be two of us."

She peered behind me as if challenging my number.

"Oh, he's not here yet."

"Would you like to sit now?" I nodded and motioned toward the back.

I slid into the booth at the very back and wondered if the magician would appear. I had had such bad luck with 99s, I expected him to be another no-show. If he did show, would he be one of those card-trick-up-the-sleeves guys or sleight-of-hand-now-you-see-it-now-you-don't types? Would his magic feature bandanas and marbles, or top hats, white gloves and rabbits? Would I have to feign wonderment when he performed his tricks, only to break the bad news to him? No,

I wouldn't reveal on the first date that he needed a real profession if he wanted to be with me.

In the meantime, I'd focus on my breath and meditate. I had been advised by just about everyone—including my boss—that I needed to meditate to become more centered, more self-assured. It's bad when you're summoned to your boss's office and you anticipate a raise or a promotion but instead, she doles out personal advice.

"Fiona, if I were you, I'd give either meditation or medication a try."

Is it that obvious? I pinched my eyes closed and focused on my in-breath, out-breath, in-breath, out-breath, but if you've ever tried it, you know it is tedious as hell. My mind gets bored and makes shit up like picturing the magician as a serial killer whose dates appear in his magic shows in the table-sawing segment. But instead of doing abracadabra: *here's the magic-show lady all safe and sound*; he actually saws you in half. And that's how your life ends—in halves.

When I opened my eyes abandoning my mindfulness practice, the magician was across from me in the booth. As were the parrot and the wand. And the patch. *Damn.*

"Why does he wear a patch?" I asked.

"She."

"Oh, sorry. How do you distinguish between males and females?"

"Females tend to be more aggressive and bite more. You know, like humans."

"I don't bite unless provoked."

"Good to know," he said with a forlorn smile.

"Why does she wear a patch?"

"She's a pirate," said the magician.

"Who's ever heard of a lady pirate?"

"Oh, there have been plenty."

"Does she want to be a pirate?" I said.

"Who doesn't?"

"Not me. I'd be perpetually seasick, peg-legs scare me, and pirate talk is so kitschy. 'Sink me! Ahoy thar. It's time to walk thee plank.'"

"A pirate doesn't have to talk like that."

"Does she talk like that?"

He shook his head and gazed at his parrot ruffling her feathers. "We worked on it for years. She could never learn."

As ridiculous as it was to be sad about a parrot who couldn't learn to talk like a pirate, I could sense his regret. As a magician he was perhaps accustomed to manipulating the world at will or at least giving the illusion of doing so.

"And the wand? Do you always take it with you?"

He nodded. "You never know when you're going to need to change what's in front of you."

I laughed nervously wondering if he felt compelled to change me. I didn't want to become a parroted pirate or a pirated parrot or any other creature requiring a patch. "So, is this what you do for a living—the magician thing?"

"It's how I've made a life."

The way guys answer when they're poor. His eyes were like kaleidoscopes with shifting patterns of beads, pebbles, and bits of glass in purple, blue, green, and yellow. I could have watched them for hours, but I didn't want to be rude or prematurely intimate, especially not with a one-eyed parrot staring me down. For all I knew, she'd squawk embarrassing things and everyone in the restaurant would crane their necks.

"But, I mean, do you make money, you know, doing magic tricks?"

"You don't need money with magic."

"So how do you pay for things like dinner at a restaurant?"

"I don't worry about that."

Perfect. He's one of those guys who has no problem using other peoples' money. "Shall we order?"

"No need to. Our food is on its way."

I laughed again, this time a high-pitched titter. I wished it had been more guttural and commanding. This guy seemed more delusional by the minute. Despite being mesmerized by his kaleidoscope eyes, I was ready to cross him off my list and surrender to the triple digits.

Sure enough; seconds later, piping hot bowls of bi bim bap and heaping servings of kimchee arrived at our table. I glanced at the server, at the magician, then at the food, trying to piece it all together. "Hey, how'd you do that?"

He responded by diving into his meal. I guessed he never answered questions about magic. No true magician did. Nothing seemed to faze this guy. If nothing else, I could use a dose of his unfazedness.

As my question dissolved into silence, the pirated parrot took flight high above the patrons—a spectacular flash of green, yellow, and orange. She was a confident but lopsided flyer; I couldn't help but blame the patch. I wanted the magician to remove it, but I didn't want to interfere with the parrot's nautical identity. Of course, she'd dream of life at sea when she was better suited to being a pilot. But do parrots dream?

Diners exclaimed and pointed at the bird. I thought we'd be chastised for our parrot or quickly escorted out. Then I noticed the parrot was flying with red roses in her beak and delivering a fresh red rose to each table, sliding it into skinny glass vases and flying to the next table with flourish. Not only were customers not perturbed with an aviary addition to their dining experience; they were delighted.

She landed, perched in the middle of the restaurant, and squawked, "Sniff your rose, people. Sniff your rose." And surprisingly everyone did. They picked up the vases and inhaled their roses. The solo red flowers exploded into bouquets of lilacs, tulips, orchids, hydrangea, and narcissus. Patrons' faces lit up with curious glee and a hint of ecstasy. Some even cheered.

For some reason, I had no faith that my nose would turn my rose into a bouquet. Sensing this, the magician reached out, grasped the vase, and held it up to my nose.

I shook my head and pushed the rose away. "It's not going to work for me."

"Why are you special? It worked for everyone else."

"That's just it. I'm not."

"Do you believe in magic?"

"I guess not when it comes to me."

"You don't have to believe in you. Just believe in me." He held the rose under my nose.

I closed my eyes and sniffed as hard as I could, thinking that the force of my inhalation might make up for any inadequacy in me. The divine rose scent delighted my nose and blossomed in my mind. But I was afraid to open my eyes.

"Look, Fiona. Look, Fiona," said the parrot.

I was so stunned that the parrot knew my name, my eyes flew open. My suspicion had been right. My rose hadn't blossomed into a bouquet of flowers like everyone else's. It had bloomed into a dozen red balloons, each marked with the number 99. I inhaled my astonishment. I hadn't told him his number.

He offered me the balloons. "Take these outside, don't let go, and you'll soon discover what stars are made of." He stroked his beard making it even more pointed than it already was.

Are you kidding me? "Only if you come with me," I said.

"No, you need to learn to trust on your own. The sky will carry you if you just let it."

As he handed me the balloons, I felt the upward tug in my trembling grasp and buoyancy in my heart. I didn't know if I'd ever make it to 100, but it didn't matter. When the world was this magical, you stopped counting.

Cabin Pressure

Bree gave him her heart; he gave her organic veggies. During their break-up, Marcus said he felt used because she insisted that he meet her high organic food standards. Not wanting to ingest pesticides, herbicides, and the other cides constituted high standards?

Bree brushed her teeth contemplating Marcus feeling used because of organic veggies. Had she known the extent of his stinginess, she might not have wasted the last ten years of her life. *STOP!* Her therapist insisted that she practice thought-stopping about the break-up with Marcus.

"Counterproductive," her shrink said. "You were with him for a reason."

Bree was still searching for the reason.

"You were with him for exactly as long as you needed to be. You two had karma to work through."

Bree wasn't sure she believed in karma, but if she did, the only karmic explanation she could come up with was learning to live with a toupee—a hairpiece, as Marcus insisted she call it. She preferred to call it Elvis. Elvis would randomly appear on top of toilets, counters, fridges, vases, and tables. It would slip sideways on Marcus' head, over his eyes, and slide back so his hairline was half-way up his scalp. From the Beatles to Donald Trump in one fell-swoop.

Marcus' greatest fear in life was not dying or public speaking but being outed as a toupee-wearing bald man. As Bree flossed, she rolled her eyes at the thought of his secret fear. Of course, any observant person could detect the fake hair effect. Marcus was so mortified by the possibility of being outed that he always kept his blinds drawn in his home.

"Can't we have a little natural light in here?" Bree would plead. Not that he knew any of his neighbors. It was just the fear of anyone's eyes catching a glimpse of his shiny, bald head with hair islands encircling each ear. He was more passionate about being an in-the-closet baldy than anything else in his life—except for bacon, lettuce, and tomato sandwiches. Although he was a gourmet cook, his favorite "recipe" was the BLT. Bree often wondered if the BLT could be called a "recipe," but she dared not ask.

Bree moved more closely to the mirror to inspect her pores and wrinkles. And her least favorite part of being a

182

middle-aged woman: the chin sprouts. As she plucked, guilt crept in. Was it wrong to insist upon organic? Did that place an undo financial hardship on Marcus and his daughter, Amelia? *STOP!* Her therapist also advised her to use thought-stopping with ruminations and regrets.

After the plucking, Bree applied bronze-glow. Why was she getting dolled up for the nine-hour plane ride to Paris? It made her feel better about hurling through space over a vast ocean in a cylindrical tin can. If she became fish food, at least she would know she went out in style.

While applying her mascara, she noticed that the house was uncharacteristically quiet. Socrates, her parrot, always squawked and made a racket, breaking up the monotony of silence. After the medieval torture of eyelash curling, Bree ran downstairs to make sure Socrates was OK. She slowed before reaching his cage, thinking if she didn't get too close, what she saw from afar might not be real. Her beloved parrot was a heap of feathers at the bottom of the cage. Bree fell backwards onto her couch and leaned her head against the wall. Then she shot up with an epiphany. Marcus had broken into her house the night before to return her tampax, underwear, bras, PJs, jewelry, skis, and ski helmet. He also rummaged through her night table and scoured every surface looking for her engagement ring and an electronic crossword puzzle gizmo her sister had given them for Christmas. (Bree never said he could have it.) He had left roses—cheap ones from Safeway—so she wouldn't be mad about the break-up break-in.

But the breaking and entering and the returning of the possessions wasn't the nature of Bree's epiphany. She had connected the dots that led to Socrates' demise. In a fit of fury, Marcus had ransacked her home and poisoned her parrot. Marcus and Socrates had a mutual disdain for one another. Socrates was the one outsider who knew Marcus' secret, and he would squawk the truth with a vengeance. "Marcus is a baldy. Marcus is a baldy." Bree accused Marcus of transient paranoia when he accused her of putting ideas in Socrates' head. "Rubbish," she said, "Socrates can reach his own conclusions."

Bree's tears were hijacked by rage as revenge fantasies flooded in. She would set up hidden toupee webcams in Marcus' home for the world to see. Seven billion people poised to witness the adventures of Marcus' hairpiece on the toupee-cam.

Out of the corner of her eye, she noticed the time—7:00 pm. She had to be at the airport in one hour. But what would she do about Socrates? If she left him, he would decompose while she was away. Bree could ask the bird sitter to bury him. No. She was a bird sitter, not an aviary funeral director. Then it struck her that she had to have an autopsy done on

Socrates. She would bring charges against Marcus—the parrot poisoner. He would regret he ever mentioned organic veggies.

With an autopsy in mind, there was only one obvious stopgap measure—the freezer. Bree reached into the cage and carefully pulled out Socrates' fragile frame and limp feathers. He had given her so many years of chirpy perkiness. She couldn't believe after all they had been through, she was now going to seal him in a Ziploc bag and slide him into the freezer. She placed him on the rack with the Popsicles and stared at him, frozen air escaping. Poor Socrates. She shivered and closed the door.

How could Marcus do such a thing? She decided right then and there that she would never, ever give her heart to another man.

Stepping onto the plane, Bree spotted a painted lady, a damsel in distress, with a colossal suitcase and a helpful man lugging and hurling the massive bag into the overhead compartment. A skeptical onlooker said, "It will never fit." As restless travelers bottlenecked in the belly of the plane, a flight attendant intervened and whisked the suitcase away.

Bree noticed that her seat was next to the skeptical onlooker. She was thrilled that she was in the third row—no more overhead compartment projects to endure. As she situated herself—stowing, sitting, buckling—she noticed that the skeptic was a man with thick lustrous salt-and-pepper hair, deep violet eyes, and juicy lips. The sight of him made her heart jump. With him as her seatmate, she realized she had picked an inopportune time to swear off men. As she adjusted her seatbelt—a four hundred pound passenger must have preceded her—he flashed Bree a broad, dimpled smile and said, "Audronis."

"Sorry?"

"Au-dro-nis," he said, extending his hand in greeting.

She laughed. "Really? Like Adonis with an 'R'?"

"Pretty much."

"What kind of name is that?" Bree asked.

"Lithuanian."

"Wow. I've never met a guy with a Lithuanian name before."

"And you?"

"Bree."

"As in the cheese?"

"Right. Would you like crackers with that?" Bree held up her hand in a waitressing gesture.

"I'll bet we've both had our fill of those lines."

She nodded. "So, Audronis, what's your story?"

"I guess you could say I'm in transition." He said nearly swallowing his words.

"Me, too."

"What are you transitioning from or to?"

"From a toupee-wearing parrot murderer."

"Wow! So, you've left your husband? Good for you!"

"Fiancé, actually. Why good for me?"

"Most guys deserve to be left. My humble opinion. And if you had the courage to leave, I say more power to you."

"Have you been left?"

He threw his head back and laughed. "Oh, more times than I'd like to count. But mostly I do the leaving."

"A player."

"A *recovering* player."

"Is there a 12-step program for players?"

"There should be. Maybe I'll start one."

"Like, hi, I'm Audronis. I've played 100 women. I'm a centurion."

"Sadly, it's more like a millenion, if that's a word."

Bree's mouth was agape.

"What about you? Are you a player? You're certainly stunning enough to be."

Bree touched her cheek and giggled. *Oh, god, did I just giggle?*

"No, a serial monogamist. I can't multi-task when it comes to men."

A flight attendant with a frosted updo, fake eyelashes, and thick blue eye shadow appeared with her cart. "Drinks for you two?"

"Yes, a gin and tonic. Make it a double, please," Audronis pulled out his wallet.

"Miss?"

"Order anything. Drinks are on me," he flashed a Platinum American Express card.

"Merlot. Do you have a Merlot?" Bree asked.

The flight attendant and her updo nodded. As she poured and mixed, Audronis and Bree sat in familiar stranger silence.

Reaching for their drinks in plastic cups, he said, "Not used to drinks in plastic."

"Don't fly much?" Bree asked.

"No, I'm usually in first class."

"Why the downgrade?"

"Oh, I'm involved in a different gig now."

"I see. Which is?"

"I was an art dealer."

"Interesting. And now?"

"Long story. What about you, Bree?"

"I dabble."

"Mysterious."

"Graphic design, painting, sculpture. A lot of candelabras."

"Why candelabras?"

"I've been trying to figure that out. Maybe you can help me crack the code."

"Something I'm known for, actually," Audronis said with a smirk.

"Not sure I want to know what that means."

"Let's see. Is there a certain darkness inside you that you're trying to illuminate?"

"God. Pretty damned perceptive for a man."

"I've seen that darkness, and it is me."

"So what's your fix then?"

"Who said it's fixed?"

"Good point. 130 candelabras later and mine's still not fixed," Bree said.

"Maybe you need a different medium or a different subject."

"What are you suggesting?"

"I'm not sure."

"What have you tried? I mean to address the darkness business?" she asked.

"Being a musician."

"What do you play?"

"You already know."

"I do?"

"Yes."

"It's like a standing bass, only smaller."

"A cello? Violin?"

"It's alive. I wrap my arms around it, hold it between my legs, and move my bow back and forth across the strings until it sings an enchanted melody."

Bree finally got it and felt simultaneously embarrassed by her slow wit and his suggestive imagery. It was suddenly very hot. Bree's face was flushed and she felt a surge between her legs. "Riiight. So, when a *recovering* player is playing, is there a code word for danger zone?"

He laughed a deep belly laugh and took a long sip of his gin and tonic. She sipped her wine and stared at the in-flight magazine peeking out of the chair pocket.

"It strikes me that you don't need any more candelabras," he said.

"Why?

"You are one."

"Oh, god, stop already. You don't even know me."

"Seriously, remember I'm a connoisseur, if nothing else. I've seen enough to know."

"I don't know." As her heart melted in the presence of this stranger, Socrates was chilling in the freezer. Her heart hadn't felt such stirrings since she first met Marcus over a decade ago. It was as if her heart had fallen into a slumber and now was being awakened by a prince—just like in the fairytales. Adonis. Audronis. How she could imagine calling out his name.

They both nodded off for a while and when she awoke, she noticed his seat was empty. She brushed the sleep out of her eyes and then spotted a note on her tray.

"Meet me in the back restroom on the right. Knock twice. Pause. Knock twice again."

Oh, my god. Without missing a beat, she pulled out her mirror and tidied up her hair and face. She popped a mint into her mouth to freshen her breath. *Oh, my god.* She unbuckled and sprung up out of her seat, noticing that most of the passengers were dozing.

She followed the knocking instructions, and sure enough, Audronis appeared behind the sliding door. He pulled her in with his mouth, deeply kissing her, sucking her tongue, licking and biting her lips. Audronis reached underneath her blouse and cupped her breasts. He squeezed and massaged her nipples, sending ripples of pleasure down to her core. Her legs felt weak. He had closed the toilet lid and directed her to sit down. He lifted her skirt and pushed her panties to the side, slipping his tongue between her legs. Bree gasped and then covered her mouth.

"It's OK. The engine noise drowns most of it out." He caressed her with his tongue and lips while gently rocking her body. She closed her eyes, threw her head back, and moaned softly—the pitch beginning to crescendo. He rocked her more intensely and before she knew what was happening, he had entered her, slowly. She gasped and moaned more loudly now. Audronis cradled, rocked, and whispered a lullaby. Bree could sense his sweet hot breath on her neck. She braced against her contractions—in an effort to muffle her moans. She was never adept at silent sex.

"Let go," he whispered, "No one will hear, except for me and I won't be able to stop myself once I hear you."

At this, she let go and a ripple starting in her womb emanated outward like a stone tossed into a still lake.

The plane taxied to its gate and Bree struggled to come up with the right parting words. *Would you want to exchange cell numbers? No, too collegial. Will we ever meet again? Too sappy. I have an art project I may need your help with. Too transparent. Would you like to check out the Picasso Museum together? Oh, god, an art dealer doing something as pedestrian as going to a museum? What, then?*

The words flew out of her mouth without her approval, "I'd really like to see you again."

Audronis' face lit up, but then he bit his lip and hesitated. "That would be nice. Wouldn't it?"

Bree held her breath.

"But I'm in no position to do that, I'm afraid."

Her breath escaped in a sigh. "Oh. I shouldn't have asked."

"No, no. You should have. I would under different circumstances."

Bree wanted to inquire about the circumstances.

They packed up their belongings and exchanged goodbyes.

She watched Audronis descend the stairs of the plane onto the tarmac, spotting two dashing men in suits at the bottom. They were watching him, too. Business associates, no doubt. No one was smiling. As he reached them, he hesitated and then offered both arms—a strange gesture. The man on the left clasped handcuffs around Audronis' wrists and escorted him to the black sedan parked on the runway.

Bree gave him her heart. He gave her his last taste of freedom.

The Reluctant Horse Whisperer

Camille had been terrified of horses ever since Pinto, her rent-a-horse, went on a wild tear, galloping through the dense pine woods of northern Michigan on a family outing led by Blanche, a woman who dubbed herself the "Horse Whisperer." Blanche explained in a hoarse voice with a Lucky Strike dangling from her imploding lips that sure, there were other horse whisperers, there were, but she was *the* Horse Whisperer. She claimed to communicate telepathically with horses and to know all their secrets. Whenever she revealed this, which she did to all her customers, their pleading eyes triggered a snorting laugh which, in turn, set off an emphysemic coughing fit. When she was able to speak again, Blanche would say, "Trust me, you don't want to know."

Camille's mother had requested a docile horse for Camille, having had to convince her to ride with her horse-obsessed siblings. Among other things, Camille was terrified of the gigantic teeth that emerged whenever adults urged kids to feed carrots to horses, saying, "Flat hand. Flat hand! Don't want him to eat your fingers. Do you?"

En route to Whispering Hope Stables, her mother had assured a whimpering Camille that certain horses were guaranteed to behave. Her mom should have gotten it in writing.

Pinto raced into the thick pine forest, scraping Camille against knotted balsam firs and Norways, eventually knocking her off. She went tumbling from the saddle and landed face-down on the pine forest floor, battered, bruised but not broken. Her sun-burnt freckled face had scratches that looked like the connect-the-dots game Camille's family played on the long car ride from Indianapolis to Higgins Lake. Her curly red hair was strewn with pine needles, pieces of pine cone, and sap. Camille's cat-like green eyes were bloodshot from crying.

The Horse Whisperer whipped the living daylights out of the run-away horse and continued to claim to apprehensive customers that Pinto was an easy ride.

Several weeks after her fiancé left her for a girl who was barely legal, 27-year-old Camille found herself inspecting a flyer tacked to a bulletin board in Merrimac's Natural Grocer. She sought wisdom from just about any source.

Feel broken—like you don't know whom to trust? Learn to trust again with a sentient being. Equine therapy will give you your heart and life back. Guaranteed to work or your money back. —The Horse Whisperer

Camille sought a guarantee, and something felt right about facing her greatest fear—horses—by learning to trust again. Eyeing the flyer adorned with naked cherubs riding winged lavender horses, she dialed the number, and a woman with the voice of someone on a 1-800-psychic hotline answered.

"Blessings from the Horse Sanctuary."

"Hi. I'm calling to—"

"Learn how to trust again."

"How did you know?"

"Horse sense. What's your name, dear?"

"Camille."

"My name is Anastasia, which is Greek for resurrection. I chose it in a renaming ceremony, because that's essentially what I do with my equine shamans."

"I should tell you right off the bat, I'm afraid of horses."

"Of course you are."

"Why of course?"

197

"Most people are. They think it's because they're afraid of falling off, but it's something entirely different, which you'll come to understand."

"I will? Can't you just tell me now?" People had been keeping secrets from her all her life.

"No, dear, you must learn it for yourself. Here's how I work. During the first session, you'll observe as I align the horse with my spirit guides. You'll watch the dynamics between us. The second session, we'll introduce you in the ring, and I'll stand back, intervening if necessary. The third session, you'll ride blindfolded—"

"Excuse me. Did you say blindfolded?"

"Yes, no worries. I'll be closely supervising your ride. And then, at last, we'll do your break-through ride."

"I'm afraid to ask."

"Don't be. You're breaking through to the spirit realm while riding naked and blindfolded. It's a rebirth, so being in your original state is critical, as is seeing with your spirit and not your eyes. The visual cues are distracting when your vision should be turned inward and upward."

Camille heard nothing after "naked and blindfolded." She broke out in nervous laughter. "I don't think so."

"Camille, I understand your hesitation, but everyone who has done it, one hundred fifty-two people in all, has had a mind-blowing transformational experience. By taking this break-through ride, you show the spirit guides where you are, and they help you cross over to the life you want to live. A little side note…the blindfold you'll be wearing can only be removed by me."

Camille waited to exhale, imagining naked riding, non-removable blindfolds, spirit guides, crossing over, and horse whisperer number two. The last time she had trusted a horse whisperer, things had gone terribly wrong. But maybe she had come full circle and was meant to do this. *I can't feel any worse than I do now.* "What do I have to lose?"

"Brilliant, Camille. You'll never be the same."

Arlen and Woody were patrolling in a squad car, doing the late afternoon beat on Elm Street in Merrimac. Arlen was ribbing Woody about his espresso stop. He was incensed by the opening of an espresso shop in Merrimac. He said it was the beginning of the end. Soon the big city folks with their high and mighty attitudes would come waltzing into town, buy up all the property and make prices go sky-high, driving out the good folk of Merrimac.

"Real lawmen don't drink expresso," Arlen said rubbing his shiny bald head in consternation.

"Well, then maybe I'm not a real lawman. Ever thought of that?" Woody's bushy salt-and-pepper mustache displayed foamed milk. "And it's esss-presso, not expresso."

"Woo-wee, Woody's going all high and mighty on me. If you didn't have that uniform on, and I saw you sipping expresso the way you are right now, I'd never have guessed you were a sheriff."

"Good. Better for undercover ops."

"Suppose so, although we don't see many cases that need 'em. Only your run-of-the-mill domestics, DUIs, and delinquents. The triple-D threat of small town, USA."

"Probably 'cuz we're so good. We keep things under control," Woody raised his espresso, toasting Merrimac's precinct.

"Uh-huh. But that expresso thing. I don't know."

Woody was ready to move on from the espresso commentary. Who gave a rat's ass that Arlen didn't approve? "You know, it's a good thing we've got everything under control. Who wants a serial killer on the loose, terrorists underfoot, or an unsolved grisly murder that haunts our town? If you want that stuff, you're one sick pup."

"I didn't say I wanted that. I'm just saying it gets a little snoozerville around here. Warning jaywalkers and non-seatbelt wearin' folks. What do we have all this gear for anyway? Don't you think it's overkill?"

"Just in case. Even small town folks can go postal and shoot up a school, a Walmart, or a church, for God's sake. Happens every day across America. You know it and I know it. You'd have to have lost your last marbles to open fire in a church with sweet old ladies and children and God watchin' overhead."

Arlen nodded, clearly distracted by his partner's lattéed mustache and still convinced he was witnessing the downfall of Merrimac right next to him in the squad car.

The radio static cleared, and the dispatcher's voice said, "We've got a 685 in the Elk Avenue neighborhood. Arlen and Woody, this one's yours. Over."

On hearing a code that was theirs, Arlen reached for his cap and slid it on, back to front.

Arlen and Woody exchanged glances, hoping the other knew what a 685 was. Woody was the first to come clean. He licked his milky mustache and picked up the radio.

"What's a 685? Over."

The dispatcher said, "A horse exposure. Over."

"Good God! A what? Over," said Woody.

"We've got a nude woman on a horse. Over," clarified the dispatcher.

Arlen wasn't going to fall for that one, so he played along. "I suppose her name is Godiva. Over."

"Oak and State Streets. Black stallion. Reportedly moving north at a nice clip. Over."

"I think this is for real, Wood."

Flipping on the flashers and siren, Woody pulled a squealing U-turn. The squad car zipped over to the intersection of Oak and State.

Godiva on her black stallion was galloping down the wrong side of Oak Street toward town. There was a mini-traffic jam in a town that knew no traffic delays. Pedestrians, strangers only seconds before, were now bonding with a chorus of exclamations. "Well, I've never!" "Now I've seen everything!" "Someone, do something!"

Inside the squad car, a duet of surprise played out. Arlen said, "Would you look at that? My, my, we've indeed got a Lady Godiva on our hands. Blindfolded and all. S'pose this is someone's fantasy gone terribly wrong? I've heard about this sorta thing among city slickers, but never in Merrimac."

"Weren't you saying things needed a little spicing up around here?

"I can't wait to see how you're going to handle this one, Wood."

"Who says I'm handling it?" Woody countered as he polished off his latte and smacked his lips.

"Divvying up the workload. I took the last one," said Arlen.

"You get a California stop. I get Lady Godiva."

"Luck of the draw."

"Holy guacamole shitoly cannole." Woody eased the car in front of the horse to block its passage, ejected himself from the squad car, and approached Lady Godiva and her horse. Arlen shadowed him, anxious to witness Lady Godiva's arrest and get an up close and personal peek at her privates, before they had to cover them by law.

"Afternoon, ma'am. I'm Officer Schultz." Woody approached the horse and held up his badge. Not that Godiva could see it. The horse halted and stood at attention, swatting flies with his tail.

"Let me explain. It's not what it looks like. You see, I was doing my breakthrough to the spirit realm ride with Anastasia over at the Horse Sanctuary and Aethenoth got spooked and took off." The peachy-skinned rider covered her breasts with one hand and grasped the reins in the other. She must have realized that straddling the saddle naked might give the wrong impression, because she whipped her legs around and crossed them, striking a sidesaddle pose.

"Uh-huh." Woody rolled his eyes at Arlen and made a coo-coo crazy sign with his finger swirling next to his head. "First things first." But Woody had no idea what came first. The naked lady needed to come down off the horse, but should they cover her and help her down, or help her down and then cover her?

"Arlen, get a blanket for this young lady." When Woody noticed the crowd encroaching, he signaled with his billy club for them to move on out. They dispersed, as ordered, but their heads didn't go in the direction of their departing bodies; their eyeballs stayed glued to the naked spectacle.

Woody was having his own eyeball management issues; they kept sneaking a peek at her breasts, which she obscured unsuccessfully with her hand. The whole scene was arousing him, which was highly inappropriate for a patrolman on duty. He gave himself credit for not lingering too much around the crotch region. Despite that, his aroused state was interfering with his intervention analysis, as in, how to get the lady down off the horse without becoming more aroused.

Arlen interrupted Woody's muddled thinking process with the blanket pass-off. "Wood, here's the blanket. Now let's cover this gal up and bring her on down."

"Good thinking, Arlen." Not really good thinking per se, just thinking period.

Woody looked up while trying to avert his eyes and said, "Miss, here's a blanket for you to cover up with. After you've done that, we'll bring you down."

"Ask her to remove the blindfold, Wood."

"Right." Woody was kicking himself for not thinking of that first. "Miss, please remove the blindfold. Then I'll hand you the blanket."

"Well, you see, officer, I can't. Anastasia is the only one with the key."

Arlen elbowed Woody, who, upon hearing that had lost complete control of the arousal factor. His stiff uniform pants were getting awfully toasty and cramped. Boot camp simulation hadn't prepped him for on-the-spot thinking while detaining a naked horseback rider.

Sizing up the situation with his stymied partner, Arlen intervened and grabbed the blanket. "Miss, I'm handing you a blanket. I'm going to need you to wrap it around you good and tight for the transition to your land legs. Copy?"

"Yes, sir." She did as instructed and Arlen coached and assisted her down.

Woody was relieved to not have to play Lady Godiva's knight in shining armor at that moment because he was feeling more weak-kneed than knightly.

"We're going to need you to remove the blindfold, miss. I'm guessing you can do it yourself unless the sorceress put some kind of spell on it."

Woody scowled at Arlen.

"Anastasia told me she's the only one who can remove it," said Camille.

"I think she meant that figuratively. Can you really trust anything that woman says?" Arlen asked.

Camille reached behind her head and fumbled with the blindfold. Woody stepped in to help her unfasten it. She scanned the scene—cop car, gawkers from afar, a horse, her nakedness wrapped in a blanket. She looked as though she would have opted for an invisibility cloak instead.

"Miss, what's your full name?" asked Arlen.

"Camille Sheehan."

"Miss Sheehan, we'll need to take you in for questioning."

"What about the horse?" she asked.

"We've got that covered." They didn't really, but that was the usual police response for "I don't know."

"But he's a wild stallion on the loose. I'm not sure anyone can control him."

Woody peered at Aethenoth, who was as stationary as a statue and watching him through his forelock. Of the pair, Camille was the only one who seemed wild and untamed.

"I know he doesn't seem that way now, but, believe me, he hightailed it out of the stable."

"Maybe he was spooked by something," guessed Woody.

"I think it's just me. I have a bad track record with horses."

Arlen gestured to Woody, who was composing himself in the shadow of the horse. "Wood, can you go ahead and cuff her?" Just when Woody had started to feel like an officer in control, the idea of cuffing Godiva set him off again. He blushed and fumbled to get the cuffs from his belt. He had never felt so butter-fingered in all his years with the force.

"Miss Sheehan, if you would, p-p-p-lease put your hands behind your back."

She obeyed, careful to keep the blanket from falling. With the sound of the lock, she started to cry.

"I'm sure your story will check out. These are just standard procedures for this sort of situation." Woody was still making a great effort to look her in the eyes.

Arlen wasn't as convinced. His voice deepened and boomed with authority. "Miss Sheehan, you do realize the potential severity of your actions. You could be charged as a sex offender, an offense that will follow you around wherever you go. Now get her into the vehicle, Woody. I'm going to call in reinforcements to deal with the horse."

Tears ran down Camille's cheeks. Perhaps she would walk away with a different lesson than intended: Never trust anyone, human or otherwise, again.

The threesome sat in a dingy, grey interior room at the Merrimac police station with cement blocks for a wall and a track of fluorescent lighting, casting a pale green glow on the interrogation proceedings. They had outfitted Camille in an orange prison jumpsuit five sizes too big. Camille bowed her head and pretzeled her arms against her chest.

Wanting to infuse cheer into an otherwise somber occasion, Woody served coffee and donuts. "Camille, please help yourself to a donut with sprinkles."

"I'm not hungry."

Seeing that Woody was soft on Camille and losing his professional edge, Arlen jumped in. "Miss Sheehan, as you no doubt know, public nudity is punishable by law. In some cases, it leads to being charged with a sex offense, along the lines of streaking, flashing, and what not. The offense is called indecent exposure, sexual misconduct, public lewdness, or public indecency. It is a criminal offense in all 50 states and is punishable by fines and/or imprisonment, and in some states a conviction results in having to register as a sex offender. In this country, unlike I-talian or Frenchy countries, we aren't big on exposing our privates in public. There's a reason they're called privates. If they were called publics, then maybe all of this hippie nudity stuff would be legal."

"Let's begin." Woody pressed the Record button on the recording device. "Camille Sheehan, what were you doing today?"

"I was completing my breakthrough to the spirit ride when everything went haywire."

"What is that, exactly?" asked Woody.

"It's a ride on a horse to learn how to trust again. Supposedly the spirit guides find you and help you live the life you were meant to live."

Arlen shook his head and asked, "And what is the point of doing the ride blindfolded and in the buff?"

"It was Anastasia's crazy plan. I thought it was ridiculous when I first heard about it, but she convinced me that it would restore my trust in people. And horses. What a crock!"

"Who's Anastasia?" asked Woody.

"The Horse Whisperer."

"And this so-called Horse Whisperer put the blindfold on you?"

"Yes, sir."

After several minutes of silence during which Arlen's fears of his town going to hell in a handbasket were only confirmed, he asked, "What is the point of all this?"

"To learn how to trust after I found my fiancée with an 18-year-old girl."

"And riding naked on a horse is allegedly going to help you get over this?" Arlen snorted in disbelief, thinking, it takes all kinds. He just wished all kinds weren't corrupting his town.

"Do you have a better idea, sir? What would you recommend after learning a few months before my wedding that the love of my life had found a teenage replacement? I already had my wedding gown!"

Woody motioned to Arlen to join him outside the deposition room. "Arlen, can you go easy on her? The poor girl's in distress. I understand it's important to follow procedures, but can we soften our approach just a little?"

"Sounds like this horse-whisperer person gave her a load of hooey. Godiva's naïve and gullible, but she broke the law nonetheless. We have to gather enough evidence to determine whether this is a case of indecent exposure."

"According to my understanding of the law, it must be shown that she knowingly exposed her genitals to the view of any person and that the exposure likely caused affront or alarm to someone. I would say the onlookers were more amused than alarmed. Wouldn't you?"

"Listen, Wood, seems you've got the hots for Lady Godiva. I don't blame you one bit. But you need some professional objectivity. This case has to proceed like any other. You and I must safeguard this town by seeing that people abide by the laws. And when they're broken, we step in. No exceptions."

When Arlen and Woody finished taking Camille's statement, Woody gave her his card. "If you need anything."

Woody was assigned to question Anastasia about the events of the Godiva incident, which was splashed on the front page of the *Merrimac Daily* and was the talk of the town in diners, pie shops, and the Espresso Stoppe. Anastasia's horse whispering operation was under increasing scrutiny for violating public nuisance laws. Woody was feeling protective of his seemingly innocent charge and wanted to see justice carried out on her behalf.

As Woody approached the Horse Sanctuary, he witnessed a rider soaring over a series of jumps, each higher than the previous. He didn't know much about riding, but this person looked like a pro, like the equestrians he had seen competing on television.

This must be her. He wasn't sure how to interrupt the Horse Whisperer at work, so he stood motionless outside the ring.

Woody watched as the horse completed its last jump then reared up and tore around as though he was spooked. The horse reared several more times, until the rider fell to the ground with a dusty thump. Woody ran over to her to make sure she was OK. When she saw she wasn't alone, she seemed defensive. He leaned over to help her up and she waved him away. A marking on the woman's neck caught Woody's eye. He couldn't quite make it out. It was a ring around her neck—almost resembling a rope burn.

"I'm fine. I'm used to it by now," she said, brushing off the dirt from her riding pants.

When the horse saw Woody, he slowed to a cantor and halted. The horse's ears tilted forward and he dropped his head toward Woody.

Woody stroked his mane.

"Anastasia, I presume?"

She nodded.

"Officer Schultz."

"How did you do that?" Anastasia asked, pointing first to the horse and then to him.

"Do what?"

"Ground his wild spirit and connect Aethenoth with his ancestors so that he's ready to communicate with humans."

"The horse, you mean?"

"Yes, the horse. When they drop their heads like that, they're signaling that they're ready to communicate with humans."

"Like Mr. Ed?" he snickered.

She didn't crack a smile. "What did you do?"

"I didn't do anything."

"Oh, yes you did. And if I could figure out what it was, I'd pay good money for it."

"That was impressive—the jumping. Where'd you learn to do that?"

"It comes naturally. I'm the Horse Whisperer." She put her hands together in prayer and bowed.

Woody wasn't a horseman by any means, but if she was the Horse Whisperer, then he was the Lone Ranger.

"Come into the ring with me."

"Well, actually I'm not here for communing with horses. I'm here to question you about the incident with Ms. Sheehan."

"Oh, that can wait."

When her eyes locked onto his and commanded him to comply, he inched into the ring.

"Now, stand by this horse. Don't touch him; just stand near him and put your hands out—palms up."

"With all due respect, ma'am, I'm not here for horse whispering lessons. I'm here to get your testimony so we can move forward with this case."

Anastasia grabbed him by the arm—positioning him next to the horse. "OK, now just stay open."

"To what?"

213

"What he tells you, of course."

"You're telling me that the horse is going to talk to me? Sorry, I don't speak horse."

The horse walked over to Woody and stared at him with one eye, then swung his head around to look at him with both eyes—straight on. He raised his head up, shook it, and then whinnied at Woody.

Anastasia in her artful riding ensemble darted over to the duo, grabbed both of Woody's hands and held them like a priest might do with grieving parishioner. "So, did you get that?"

"Listen, this is ludicrous. I told you I don't speak horse."

"OK, but if you did, what would he have said? He was communicating with you, but I couldn't access the lines of communication. I was locked out."

"He said you had better stop using him on those crazy naked rides or your business will receive a cease and desist order."

"Oh, he did not."

Dropping her hands, Woody said, "I'm going to be honest with you here. This all seems nuts. You, the horse whispering, and the torture you put Ms. Sheehan through. Now you had better get a rein on your horse services or we're going to have to shut you down. Is this the horse you assigned to Ms. Sheehan?"

Anastasia nodded.

"Listen. I don't know much about horses, but Crazy Horse here isn't the best choice for the trust-building business. You do realize that you may have achieved just the opposite effect of your business claims in the case of Ms. Sheehan?"

"That remains to be seen. Doesn't it?"

"Now let's have a seat over there on the bench so we can tape your testimony. I've got some work to do back at the station."

On their Sunday afternoon beat, Arlen noticed that Woody seemed preoccupied, more quiet and withdrawn than usual. Being the kind of guy to put two and two together, Arlen asked him while patrolling the outskirts of town, "It's Godiva. Isn't it?"

"No, I just haven't felt myself lately is all."

"Ever since the Godiva incident."

"And then the Horse Whisperer made me talk to a horse. And, you're going to think I'm totally off my rocker, Arlen, but I think I actually heard something."

"From the horse?" Arlen chuckled.

"Yeah, nutso—huh?"

"Afraid so. Certifiable."

"I know. So now I'm worried that I'm hearing voices. Think I need to see Doc Patterson?"

"Not a bad idea. There was a guy on the force who went through a near-death thing and he started hearing angels. Not long after, he thought he was the Messiah and ended up in the loony bin. While there, he thought he found Judas and tried to kill the guy with a fork, so he wouldn't be hanged and have to go through the whole resurrection deal. He said he was going to do the Jesus thing differently this time. No crown of thorns, no cross, no hanging. None of it. The forked guy lived, but he has fork-hole scars all over his body. Imagine using a fork. Gee willikers!"

Woody crossed his arms and stared straight ahead at the manicured lawns on one side and the open pasture on the other. He worried that the Horse Whisperer was turning him into a fork murderer.

"By the way, what did the horse say?"

"That the Horse Whisperer is a threat to horses."

"Doesn't that just figure?" Then, realizing he was getting caught up in loony-tunes talk, Arlen said, "If a horse could talk, that is."

After weeks of searching for a reason to contact Camille, Woody finally had a bona fide business purpose for getting in touch. When she answered, he said in his most professional sounding voice, "What I'm going to need you to do is purchase more services from the Horse Whisperer. The force will defray the costs."

"No, thank you. I've had my fill of her for a lifetime, maybe several."

"In exchange for your undercover work, we may be able to drop the sex offense charges."

"You can do that? OK, let's talk. Are you trying to shut down her business or something?"

"Something like that. Oh, and I'll be undercover."

Woody picked up Camille in an unmarked squad car. She stood outside and motioned for him to roll down the window. "Um, should I ride in the front or the back? If I ride in the back, people will think I'm under arrest. Again," she said.

"It's an unmarked car."

"Oh, trust me, people know unmarked cars. You're not as sleuthy as you think," she said.

Woody chuckled. "It's OK. You can hop in the front."

Camille hardly recognized Woody, sporting a clean-shaven face and a buzz cut. He wore jeans and a Polo shirt. "Wow! I wouldn't have known it was you!"

"That's the idea."

Camille was dazzled by all the gadgets, radios, keyboard, and computer monitor. "What's this here for? Do you surf the internet while driving?"

"Send email, instant message, all of that."

"Isn't that against the law, officer?"

"For you, but not for me. I am the law."

"Shall we turn on the siren and rush off to the scene of a crime?"

"We're not authorized to do that without a bona fide reason."

"Oh, come on. You guys do that all the time whenever you're stuck in traffic or late for dinner."

"I've only done it a few times."

Camille shot him a yeah-right glance and picked up the police radio, pretending to talk into it. "We're on the trail of the Horse Whisperer. She's wanted for being a horse thief. Over. So, is that why my charges are pending? Is she wanted for something? God knows what, though. Some indiscretion with her imaginary friends?"

"We're investigating questionable business practices— some that you're intimately familiar with."

When Woody and Camille arrived at the Horse Sanctuary, Anastasia greeted them, "Now, who's this? Your gentleman friend? Are you introducing him to the magic of equine therapy?" She was running two horses in the ring. "Camille, you want the Healing Your Heart package—right?"

What I really want is the Healing Yourself from Equine Therapy package, Camille thought.

"So what's he here for?" Anastasia seemed a little wary.

"To learn the secret art of horse whispering," said Woody.

After the session, Woody and Camille buckled up in the squad car. Camille donned his navy police hat and it slid down to her eyes. She tipped it back to address him. "So, did you get what you needed with all of that pseudo horse healing mumbo-jumbo?"

"I'm not sure."

"All you cops are alike. Can never give too much away. Do they teach you that at the police academy? You know, you seem too sweet and sensitive to be a cop. Or are you just that way around me?"

Guilty as charged. Woody blushed and squirmed in his seat. She was closing in on him.

"Have you figured out whether you can drop the charges?" asked Camille.

Woody didn't understand what was happening to him. Why did he have Lady Godiva in the squad car? Why in

God's name was he talking to horses? Was he protecting and serving the people, as he had pledged when he took the oath, by getting tips from a horse? He steered the car over to the shoulder of the road and, without saying a word, embraced Camille right there in broad daylight; his lips caressed hers while his tongue danced the tango.

Camille didn't resist. "What do you call that, Officer Schultz? Frenching in the line of duty?" Camille teased.

"I'm sorry. That was wrong of me, especially given your recent heartbreak. Listen, this is a very strange time for me. Don't worry. I won't let it happen again."

Camille looked down at her feet and hid underneath the cap. She peered at Woody and said, "You won't?"

"I could get dismissed for this transgression."

Camille's attention turned to a pair of horses on the other side of the fence. "Here's your chance, Mr. Whisperer, to show your stuff."

She and Woody got out of the car and strolled up to the horses.

"What are they saying?"

"They want you to know that we're dropping the charges," he said.

Camille flung her arms around him and thanked him over and over again.

A solemn look eclipsed his smile, and he added, "That's not all. The horses sense your fear of life."

Woody could imagine the headline, "Horse Cracks Case; Cop Cracks Up." Of course, no one would ever know he followed the horse's lead, not even Arlen. If he came clean, Arlen would think he was going the way of the fork-impaler.

Woody was back at the station, reviewing various insurance fraud cases involving horses.

Arlen snuck in and peeked over his shoulder. "You're really getting into this horse stuff big time. Haven't you had your fill?"

Woody toggled back to his monthly report. "I suppose you're right. I think I'll give it a rest for a while."

Arlen lingered while Woody was anxious to get to the bottom of the horse nonsense, fueled by a desire to confirm that his sanity was in check.

The communiqués from Aethenoth were repeated messages of "horse dynasty gets away with murder" and "Anastasia isn't who she says she is." With this tip-off, Woody started researching horse dynasties. At times, he tilted back in his office chair, plagued by dread that he had lost his marbles. Other times it felt entirely natural to be following leads from a horse.

After Arlen left, Woody bolted his office door and dug more deeply into an insurance fraud case with a crook named Harrington Brooks. Brooks hired an assassin named Joey "The Jumper" Torino to kill his daughter's horse, Henry Apple, for the insurance money. The horse's death deeply traumatized his eleven-year-old daughter, Eliza Jane Brooks, who was near the stable when the horse was electrocuted. Woody discovered that many involved in race horse insurance fraud chose execution by electrocution because veterinarians could wrongly determine the cause of death to be colic.

Then he came across a ten-year-old case of an heiress named Natalie Windermere. She was involved in a scheme to kill show horses for insurance money. The heiress disappeared when the scheme came to light. People believed she had gone missing in the South Pacific. Woody googled her, thinking that possibly, just possibly, Anastasia was Natalie. But he saw no resemblance. Another dead end.

One afternoon when Woody couldn't abide spanning the worlds of Doolittle and Holmes any more, he phoned Camille. "I'm sorry to bother you, but I have to tell someone. I think I'm losing it."

"What makes you think that?"

"I'm following leads from a horse. I've been over to Anastasia's several more times under the guise of learning horse whispering, and I keep receiving the same messages from Aethenoth."

"You're kidding? Now *you're* taking this horse folly seriously, too? OK, I'll play along. What is the horse telling you?"

"That Anastasia is a threat to horses."

"And a threat to people, too. I could have told you that, and I'm not even a horse. But maybe you've given up listening to humans."

"I think they're connected somehow."

"What evidence do you have?" Camille asked.

Realizing he should have been posing that question and not the other way around, he said, "No corroborating evidence, just horse whispers."

"So, basically, no evidence."

"Right."

"Wait! I have an idea. If you can talk to horses, maybe you can cure me of my horse problem? You could be the horse translator as I work through my horse shit, so to speak. And, in the process, you can get more information from this horse to clarify his cryptic messages."

"Only thing is…"

"I know. I'll have to buy another package from the Crazy Horse Lady."

"You're catching on."

Woody stayed up for three nights straight searching for leads that pointed back to Anastasia. He phoned in sick to work for the first time since he joined the force fifteen years earlier.

As Anastasia led a shiny chestnut stallion named Allegria around the ring with Camille and Woody riding together for their Trust-in-Tandem session, Woody asked, "Does Henry Apple mean anything to you?"

Anastasia flinched but kept leading the horse.

Camille glanced behind at Woody, wondering what he was up to.

"Awfully traumatic to lose your beloved horse at such a young age. Especially painful when it's your own father who ordered the killing."

Anastasia glared at Woody. "I'm sorry. I don't follow."

"Then why, if it broke your heart, did you get into the business yourself?"

Anastasia pulled on the reins and led the horse to the edge of the ring.

"And now you're hiding out in Merrimac, hoping no one will discover your real identity, Eliza Jane Brooks, alias Natalie Windermere, alias Anastasia. Did you know that changing identities only works for a time and then the law catches up with you, even if you go from horse heiress to healer? It's horses just the same. Should have gone into car racing. Gambling even."

Camille wondered if Woody's alleged animal communicating was driving him to the brink and making him wrongly accuse Anastasia. Camille didn't understand the connection between Anastasia, Eliza Jane, and Natalie, and why Woody was accusing Anastasia of something this Natalie woman had done.

Anastasia snapped. "I don't know Eliza Jane. Or Natalie Winder...for that matter."

Woody held up a police photo, labeled Natalie Windermere, with a rope scar around her neck. "A rather unique scar. Wouldn't you say? Although cosmetic surgery altered your facial structure, this scar is a dead give-away."

Camille leaned in and closely examined the scar around Anastasia's neck, the eerie rope burn marking she had noticed during her first session. She compared the scar on the woman in the photo with Anastasia's. It looked like an exact match.

"I'm sorry, Eliza Jane Brooks, but you're under arrest," said Woody, dismounting the horse, flashing his badge, pulling out some handcuffs, and locking them onto her wrists. "Painful history. I regret that it has come to this."

Although she knew she should be primarily concerned about Anastasia's welfare at that moment, Camille was now more focused on the fact that no one was tending to the horse—not the horse murderer turned horse whisperer, not the cop turned reluctant horse whisperer, just herself, the horse blunderer. The horse, also noticing that it wasn't being supervised, trotted around the perimeter of the corral. Afraid of a repeat performance of the anti-trust ride, Camille pulled on the reins. "Whoa!" she ordered. "Whoa, Allegria!"

She heard Anastasia exclaim, "It was believed that Natalie was murdered by hit men. She was planning to report the insurance fraud, but somehow they found out and tried to hang her with horse ropes to make it look like an accident."

"Natalie being you and you being Eliza Jane, that is," clarified Woody.

Allegria broke into a canter, giving Camille a bumpy ride, "Excuse me. I know you're in the middle of an arrest, but would someone please help me?"

Neither Woody nor Anastasia noticed Camille's predicament. And handcuffed, Anastasia wasn't in a position to assist with horse management anyway. That left Woody, who was wrapped up in Anastasia's arrest.

Camille shrieked as Allegria cantered out of the corral and galloped into the open field. She closed her eyes and begged for help from any spirit guides who were watching.

As Allegria stormed through the swaying prairie grass, Camille's body tensed up and braced for whatever was to come—a tumble, a fall, a throw. She was certain of one thing—this wouldn't end well.

Then Camille was struck with an insight: Fear increases gravitational pull. Living aloft requires indifference to fear.

She succumbed to the rocking motion of the stallion; the two became one entity, his torso, her thighs, his back, her pelvis, his neck, her arms, his warmth, her warmth. The same wind that whipped through his mane whipped through her hair. They traveled as one force past oak trees, willows, maples, thistles, blue flax, wild poppies, and sunflowers. At once, they cradled and soared. Out of Camille's unyielding rigidity emerged surrender to the stallion's pace, rhythm, and fluidity. Earth, hoof, body, sky.

In the space of several minutes, Camille realized that she had gone to the edge of fear, where fear couldn't be more intense and, instead of dropping off, she dropped the fear and soared.

At the outer reaches of the field, Allegria changed course and steered Camille back to the Horse Sanctuary. As Camille and Allegria reached the stables, she spotted Anastasia and

Woody outside, looking as concerned as anyone could about a breakaway horse. But when they saw Camille's exhilarated grin and flushed face, they eased up.

As Anastasia and Woody strolled toward the patrol car, Anastasia turned to Camille and said, "You did it; didn't you?" Anastasia joined her handcuffed hands in prayer and bowed.

Acknowledgements

For my beloved Z, editor extraordinaire, who never let the dream die even as life threw me a succession of curveballs.

To my dear mom for tolerating being featured in the title and the publishing of this book, one she'll likely never read. Or will she be so curious that she can't resist the urge to dive into her daughter's musings about the sensual side of human nature?

For my dad, the leader of my cheering section, who entered the spirit world before these stories were published, which may not be a bad thing. Dads don't need to know what their daughters think about sex and sensuality.

My dad heralds from a long line of literary and lawyerly types. I ditched the lawyerly legacy in favor of the literary one. I'm proud to carry on the Tinkham tradition and am hoping to pass the torch to my niece if the fancy strikes her.

To Jonathan Bitz, editor of *Denver Syntax*, who indulged my fiction-writing habit, publishing many of these stories with themes of sex, love, sperm banks, and rock and roll. He wasn't afraid to go there.

For my writers' group—Laurel, Monica, Tami, Gye, Suzanne, and Susan who provided saucy inspiration for revisions, buoying me through the lows, and celebrating the highs of the publishing journey. Save for Laurel, I miss your writerly presence in my life.

To Boulder County Independent Authors, a burgeoning group of talented authors and kindred spirits. Under the steady hand and inspired leadership of Kate Jonuska, we come together to strategize, peddle our wares, and have a jolly good time doing it.

To the folks at Lighthouse Writers' Workshop who helped me discover my love of short fiction. In 2006 I signed up for a novel-writing class, hoping I could polish off a novel I had been working on for years. On the first day, I discovered our weekly assignment was to write a short story and read it aloud. I nearly dropped out of the class. But once I surrendered to the short form, I fell in love.

To all the people in my life—good, bad, and otherwise who inspired these stories.

About the Author

Ann Tinkham is a writer based in Boulder, Colorado. She is an anti-social butterfly, pop-culturalist, virtual philosopher, ecstatic dancer, political and java junkie. When she's not tinkering with words, she's seeking adventures. Ann has talked her way out of an abduction and talked her way into the halls of the United Nations. She hitchhiked up a mountain in Switzerland and worked her way down the corporate ladder. Ann has flown on a trapeze and traded on the black market in Russia. She cycles up steep canyons, hikes to glacial lakes and mountain peaks, and blazes her own ski trails.

Her fiction and essays have appeared in many literary journals, including Foliate Oak, Slow Trains, The Adirondack Review, The Citron Review, The Literary Review, Toasted Cheese, Wild Violet, and Word Riot. Ann's essay, "The Tree of Hearts" was nominated for a Pushcart Prize and her story, "Afraid of the Rain" was nominated for Sundress's Best of the Net Anthology. Her first short story collection, *The Era of Lanterns and Bells*, was published in 2017.

CPSIA information can be obtained
at www.ICGtesting.com
Printed in the USA
LVHW091459130620
657889LV00020B/2973

9 780999 015711